In Too Deep

His smile faded a little. "I know. And Lily, I'm really sorry that I handled it so badly. This is kind of new for me."

That stopped me. Gorgeous Lucas, football star Lucas, must have had tons of girls coming on to him.

"What, exactly, is new to you?"

He waved a hand between us. "This. Us. You. Being… caring…about how a girl's feeling."

"You didn't care about other girls' feelings?" Maybe my radar about Lucas being a good guy really was off.

"Well, yeah, sure. But there was never any girl that I went out of the way to… Listen, I'm not great with words, and I know I'm going to screw up what I want to say."

"You're right. I don't want to talk about other girls in your life."

"That's just it. That's what I'm trying to say…badly. There were no other girls where I felt like this. Wondering where they were, what they were doing. And not in a stalker kind of way. But because I really cared where you were, what you were thinking, what you were feeling. It's all different with you, Lily, and…and…I don't really know what I'm doing." He sat forward, his arms once again resting on his knees. But this was not a relaxed pose; he was leaning toward me. He put a hand out as if to touch my knee, then pulled it back. "So, bear with me, okay?" he whispered.

"Okay," I whispered back, with no hesitation.

I would bear with Lucas. And, I suspected, very shortly be bare with him, too.

OTHER TITLES BY
MARA JACOBS

The Worth Series
(Contemporary Romance)
Worth The Weight
Worth The Drive
Worth The Fall
Worth The Effort
Totally Worth Christmas
Worth The Price
Worth The Lies
Worth The Flight
Worth The Burn

Freshman Roommates Trilogy
(New Adult Romance)
In Too Deep
In Too Fast
In Too Hard

Anna Dawson's Vegas Series
(Romantic Mystery)
Against The Odds
Against The Spread
Against The Rules
Against The Wall
Against The Grain

Romantic Suspense
Broken Wings

Contemporary Romance
Instant Replay

Countdown To A Kiss
(A New Year's Eve Anthology)

IN TOO DEEP

Freshman Roommates, Book One

MARA JACOBS

Published by Copper Country Press, LLC
©Copyright 2014 Mara Jacobs
Cover design by Mara Jacobs

ISBN: 978-1-940993-93-5

For more information on the author and her works, please
see www.marajacobs.com

For Every Great
Love At First Sight
Romance

ONE

·※·

I didn't believe in love at first sight, until I first saw Lucas Kade.

I WAS giving swimming lessons to at-risk kids at the pool on campus when I saw him. He sat on the old-fashioned observation area that was made of the same aquamarine tile, which surrounded the pool. Several rows up, he leaned forward, arms on his thighs, his hands clasped together. He was pretty far away, but I felt his gaze burning into me, watching me as I helped teach kicking skills to the four little kids assigned to me.

He wore a black Bribury College polo shirt and jeans. What looked like big work boots were on his feet, though the angle I was at didn't give me the best view. I couldn't tell how tall he was, but his legs seemed to go on forever. His shoulders were broad and, even leaning forward, I could see the strength in them.

I was dying to see the color of his eyes, but it was just too far away. His hair was jet black and straight, and longer than what the typical Bribury boys wore. As he leaned forward even more, the ends of his hair brushed along his jawline and I imagined how soft it would feel.

One of my students, Andy, sputtered and started flailing, his hands coming away from the wall. He went down like a rock. I calmly reached for him and lifted his little body to the surface. When I pulled him up, he looked at me with suspicion, like he knew I was watching the hot guy in the stands and not him.

He'd be right.

I patted Andy's head and gave him a "great job" as I made sure he was grasping the wall again, but my eyes turned back to Black Polo Shirt. There was a little smile playing across his lips and I swore he quirked a brow at me, almost like he knew I inadvertently let Andy go under because I was ogling his long legs and broad shoulders.

He'd be right.

Okay, I couldn't see for sure that he quirked a brow at me… but somehow I just *knew* that he did.

My heart started beating a little faster and I tried to remember if I'd seen him on campus before today, but I knew I hadn't. I would definitely have remembered him.

"And you'll never forget him," some little melodramatic voice in my head whispered.

Seriously? I don't do thunderstruck. I don't do voices in my head—at least not of the romantic sort. No, just your normal voices, like "would you please stop talking, you dumb bitch" while you smiled and nodded as the girl next to you in class droned on.

But this voice, in both the message and tone, was very different.

I'm no cynic, and I'd had a couple of semi-serious boyfriends in high school who I was hot for, but I don't ever remember this dryness in my mouth, this slight tremble in my hands, as I watched a boy watching me.

"Hey, Lily, watch me," Jessica, one of my other students, said. I turned my attention to my kids and helped them turn on to their backs.

It wasn't my first time teaching kids to swim, but I'd always done it at the country club. There, the mothers watched halfheartedly while gossiping with each other, or flaunting their newest piece of jewelry.

A very different group of mothers sat and watched this group of kids. Some were even no-shows. There was no flaunting of any kind.

I'd been at Bribury College a month. A month of making new friends and checking out the male population and realizing that, yeah, I was probably in over my head academics-wise, but I'd work my ass off to make sure my father didn't have anything to bitch about.

I always did what I had to do to keep the peace.

When the lesson finished, I switched the two boys in my group with the two girls in Freddy's group at the locker room. They wanted to have integrated groups—all part of the socialization, apparently—but obviously we at Bribury played by the rules and didn't allow boys and girls to shower together.

Not that I wasn't pretty sure that was happening on the co-ed floor below mine in the dorm.

My little girls briefly ran under the showers, still in their little-girl swimsuits of bright neon colors, just barely washing off the chlorine. I toweled off and slid yoga pants and a hoodie over my still-wet suit.

The girls would have been ready way before me otherwise, and besides, after I did the mommy-talk thing, I was going to get some real swimming in before I headed to the library and tried to get my head above the homework waters.

When all of my wards were ready, and after we did one last check and found Casey's something or other—as we inevitably did each week—I marched them all out to greet their moms, who weren't allowed in the locker room with the girls. (Again, part of the program, and, let's face it, these kids were used to doing without their moms at times. Most times. No helicopter kids, these.)

In the hallway, the boys were waiting—as they inevitably were each week—and I traded back for my boys as we made our way to the meet-and-greet area.

The moms for three of my four kids were there and I did the whole "He's coming along great. Practice having him put his face in the water in the bathtub" thing.

It was part of the gig. A couple of the instructors were doing this for credit. Like, 400-level credit. But apparently they didn't have enough students for that class, or too many kids that signed up for lessons, and needed to hire extra instructors.

I didn't really need the money, though it felt good to earn my own instead of just using the debit card my parents fed, but I knew giving swimming lessons to at-risk kids would look good.

And I always did what looked good.

Andy hung with me when all the other mothers had taken their kids and left. "Mom late again, buddy?" I asked him. There was no judgment in my voice—I had none. Or, if I'd had any, it was gone after three weeks of meeting these mothers, who were trying to do what was right for their kids, even though it couldn't have been easy to get the kids to campus, wait around for an hour, and then talk to the stupid instructor who was basically just checking off a box. "Interact with child's parent, giving meaningful feedback? Check."

"No," Andy said, but he didn't meet my eyes. He'd done that before. We'd only been holding lessons for three weeks and already his mom had flaked three times, showing up ten, twenty, even thirty minutes late. And she'd never been in the observation area like most of the moms, watching her kid. She never even partook in the after-lesson debrief with me, just waved for Andy to hurry up, shouting a "thanks" to me from down the hall. I got paid either way, so I didn't really care, but I felt bad for Andy, always running down the hallway while she waited impatiently.

I had no idea about this woman's story. Obviously if her kid was in an at-risk outreach program, there were some issues. But I thought about my mom, bringing me to every swim lesson, staying and watching through the whole thing. For years. Right through high school swim meets. Even while practicing law part-time and dealing with my father's crazy schedule.

"There he is," Andy said, pointing down the hall.

My mind was barely processing the "he" instead of "she" when it went into free fall as I watched the guy in the Bribury polo move down the hall toward us, his eyes on Andy.

And then they turned to me.

He was even more gorgeous up close, and as he moved closer still, I felt that hitch again—like I'd gone underwater without first holding my breath.

"That's my brother, Lucas. He's picking me up today, because my mom…" Andy was saying. I got the vitals: Lucas—brother. Andy might have said more, but by then the guy—Lucas—had reached us.

"You looked great out there, A. Really comfortable in the water. How'd it feel?"

Andy's little chest puffed up. "Good. Better."

Better? Had there been a problem before? Sheesh, some instructor I was.

"That's good. That's really good. See, I told you it would get better."

Andy was nodding, his fair hair wet and shaggy, droplets falling onto the back of his sweatshirt. Freddy never did help the boys with stuff like their hair in the locker room.

"Did you see me go under?" Andy asked, pride in his voice. Like it wasn't me who'd let him slip out of my hands.

"I did. Very brave. Way to conquer, my man," Lucas said. He wasn't looking at Andy now, but at me. With a look that said he knew exactly how Andy's fear had been conquered.

"Yeah, you were right, Lucas. Nothin' I couldn't handle." The words were spoken in such a way that I knew that was how they'd been sold to Andy.

"This is Lily. My teacher."

I held my hand out, but Lucas had just put his hand-shaking hand on Andy's shoulder. He just nodded in my direction. "Lily," he said slowly. "Thanks for taking such *good care* of my guy." Sarcasm dripped from his voice.

Andy was puffing up again—obviously loving that he was Lucas's "guy." But I barely noticed; my brain had gone semi-dead when Lucas said my name. His voice was smooth and deep. And dark. So, so dark.

In high school, I snuck into the school pool really late at night, had the place to myself. I did that from time to time, just to get away. I never swam, though—I was too much of a goodie-goodie to break that much of a rule. Plus the whole safety thing stopped me. But one night, after a particularly galling scene of listening to my father berate some poor flunky on the phone, I did go in.

I dove from the high board in just my bra and panties. No lights were on, and when the water swallowed me up I was cocooned in deep, wet darkness. It was disorienting, scary, and exhilarating all at the same time.

That's what it felt like when Lucas said my name.

"I'm supposed to get some information from you?" he asked me. "Like how he's doing? Stuff to work on?"

There was a tiny bit of vulnerability in his voice, which was in contrast to the sheer physical confidence he seemed to exude.

His eyes—brown, a deep, lovely shade of brown—darted between Andy and myself, and I realized he was uncertain.

"Yes," I said, summoning all my father's bullshitting skills. "Andy is indeed becoming more comfortable in the water, and that is leading to increased confidence in his abilities. I think that our next session will show even more improvement."

Lucas was nodding, but his eyes—so expressive, those brown pools, when the rest of his face was impassive—sparked with skepticism.

Yeah, people always knew when my father was bullshitting them, too.

"In the meantime," I pushed on (sadly, my father's daughter), "you could work with Andy on his floating. Easy to do in the tub. A few minutes on his back, then a few on his front, with his face to the side to breathe."

"We don't have a bathtub," Andy said.

I saw Lucas clench the hand that wasn't resting on Andy's shoulder.

"We'll figure something out, buddy," Lucas said. Andy

looked up—way up; Lucas had to be six-three—and grinned at his older brother. That grin said Andy truly believed that Lucas was capable of creating a bathtub where none existed.

Hell, maybe he was.

"We need to get going, buddy," Lucas said, turning Andy toward the exit. They started walking away. After a couple of feet, Andy turned and said with his lopsided smile, "Thanks, Lily, see you next time." He waved his little hand, his sweatshirt too large for him, the sleeve almost swallowing him up.

"You bet, Andy," I said. My hand was still raised in a wave when Lucas turned around. His gaze was intense again. My hand froze where it was—midair, mid-wave.

"Thank you," Lucas said so softly I wasn't sure if he'd actually spoken the words or mouthed them. "Lily," he added.

That word I heard. All the way through my body.

I swam laps for an hour. It was longer than what I normally did, and I pushed myself harder. I thought about the studying I should be doing. I thought about my roommates and how we were—finally—starting to gel.

But my mind kept coming back to Lucas. I knew Andy's last name was Bell from my roster. But that didn't necessarily mean Lucas had the same last name. In fact, that would be pretty rare with the kids in this program.

Bribury was an elite, Ivy League wannabe school filled with the kids of movers and shakers who didn't have quite enough moves and shakes to get their kids into Harvard or Yale. It was in a smallish town halfway between Baltimore and DC.

It was idyllic and ivy-covered (see? they've got nothing on us; our ivy grows just as thick) and small and exclusive. There was nothing but BMWs, Mercedes, and other sports cars in the student parking lot.

But the town that surrounded Bribury was—in my father's words—a complete shithole.

Crime, poverty, drugs…the Triple Crown of shitholes.

On campus, we didn't see it. And if our power-hungry parents had taught us anything, it was to not see what we didn't want to.

Unless it looked good to do so.

After swimming laps, I walked through the deserted locker room to the far corner and the old-fashioned steam room. I grabbed three of the clean towels from the bench in front, and made my way into the room I'd turned on before lessons.

I loved this steam room. It was like something out of a movie, where, like, the Ukrainian mafia discussed who was going to be "offed" or something.

I peeled out of my suit, wrung it out, and laid it on the lower tile bench. I wrapped one of the towels around me and spread another one out on the top tile bench, then sat on it. Completing the old Ukrainian man vision in my mind, I draped the third towel over my head, with a good third of it dangling in front, almost like a shroud.

Instead of thinking about who needed whacking, I thought again of Lucas. Of how his tall, muscular body moved as he'd walked down the hall toward me. Of how his hair had been so black and smooth once he'd gotten close. Of how I wished he'd gotten even closer.

I wasn't a total whore, and had only been with one boyfriend in high school, but the sight of Lucas's broad shoulders in the black polo, and his tight—I mean *tight*—ass in those jeans… Well, that sight would get even the goodiest goodie-goodie wondering if she could get away with a quick, self-administered relief session right here, in a university steam room.

I didn't, of course, but God, how my body wanted me to. Exhausted from the laps, further wrung out from the heat and steam, my limbs felt languid and liquid. Like my arms and legs might just blend into the scuzzy old tile that lined the inside of the room.

I lifted my arms to the towel on my head, gently squeezing across my breasts as I did. My legs shifted. I needed to get out of here, take a cold shower. The place was always empty this late into the evening, but still, it wouldn't do for Lily Spaulding, daughter of Grayson Spaulding, political consultant extraordinaire, to be caught diddling herself in a steam room.

Hmmm…but maybe in the shower?

I rose from the bench, the hard tile having made little dents in my ass and thighs, even through the towel.

I wrapped the towel from my head—not as sweat-and-steam-drenched as the towel I'd worn—around my body. I took the other two, and my swimsuit, and left the room, careful to turn the room off at the control panel. Nobody seemed to mind—or notice?—that I was here this late, but leaving a steam room on all night would probably curb that.

I walked out of the room, turned toward my locker, and froze.

Lucas was staring straight at me. He seemed as startled as I was, but recovered faster. A slow—God, so sexy—smile spread across his face.

"I'm here to collect the towels," he said. Then the smile turned just a little deadly and I wondered if I was about to get whacked by some fictional Ukrainian mafia boss. He nodded at my body, at my hand that clung to my barely closed towel.

"Hand it over."

TWO

❖

"WHAT ARE you doing here?" I asked, my hand clutching a bit tighter. Not so much to hang on to the towel, but as if I could cover how my body was reacting to seeing him here after I'd just been thinking about him. And about touching myself. And about how much better it would be if he were the one doing the touching.

"I'm gathering up the towels," he said. He pointed in the general vicinity of my boobs. "And I need *that* one." The smirk was gone from his face now, but it was still in his eyes.

"Are you supposed to even be in here?" I thought about the situation, about my options. I was in a locker room—in a *towel*—by myself with a strange man. I should be thinking about exit strategies, where was the nearest door, could anybody hear me scream, that sort of stuff.

But I wasn't. Somehow I knew on some gut level that I wasn't in any danger from Lucas. At least not *that* kind of danger. Because—let's be real—Lucas was dangerous, all right.

"What's your last name?" I asked, because it seemed important to know that right now. Not that standing wrapped in a towel in front of someone I'd just met (and barely, at that!) wasn't important stuff too. But…yeah… "What's your last name?" I repeated. "Is it Bell?"

There was a flash in his eyes that I couldn't read…something that made him pissed off. He grunted and broke eye contact.

Broke the spell I'd been under, and I was able to move toward my locker, a row over from where we stood.

He didn't follow me, and as I turned the corner around the aisle I looked back to see him, indeed gathering up the dirty towels that hadn't quite made it in the large laundry cart.

"No. Not Bell," he said. "Bad enough that that asshole's name is something Andy has to live with."

I opened my locker and gathered my clothes, setting them on the bench, not really knowing how this was going to work. Should I just quickly throw them on and hope Lucas stayed in the next aisle over? Keep the towel on until he left? What if he had a bunch of work to do in here and I'd be sitting in my towel for an hour?

What the hell, why was *I* the one working around *him*?

"Shouldn't you have to wait until everyone's out before you clean in here? Isn't this…I don't know…against the law, or the rules, or something?" I hitched my towel up higher around my chest, even though he was still on the other side of the lockers.

"I yelled in. There was no answer. When I saw the light on in the steam room, I was about to leave. That's when you walked out."

"Oh."

"Are you near your clothes?"

"Yes."

"Go ahead, I won't bother you. I need to do some measurements in the steam room, but I wanted it to cool down a little bit first. Thought I'd help out with the towels while I waited."

"Ummm…"

There was quiet, then he said, "I'll step out. Just yell when it's okay to come back in."

This was stupid. The man was just doing his job.

Ah, now I got why he was wearing a Bribury polo. Not so much out of collegiate pride as, well, a uniform.

And suddenly I didn't want him to think of me as a stuck-up Bribury Basic. (Which I knew was what the townies called us coeds. I learned that, like, my second day here, though I wasn't sure what it meant.)

"You can stay. Do your work. Just stay over there."

"Will do," he said. I started to change, quickly at first, then more slowly, as if daring—willing?—him to impatiently see what was taking me so long.

Yeah, pretty passive-aggressive, but I wasn't above a little p/a behavior. Sometimes it felt like my whole life was passive, with minimal aggressive.

"You about done?" he said loudly. "I've got what I needed."

I pulled my dry hoodie over my tee, shoving the wet-ish hoodie and yoga pants in my backpack. I wished there was a full-length mirror on this side of the room, but I knew what I looked like—typical college girl in jeans, tee, and sweatshirt. I put my long black hair up into a messy bun, fastening the wet mass with a band.

Typically I would have taken a long shower, but I wasn't feeling like my typical self.

"Yeah, I'm good," I said, and walked around the aisle.

He was writing something onto a small tablet, and he was holding a tape measure, which he slid into his back pocket. The door to the steam room stood open. "Me too," he said. "I got what I need." He looked me up and down. I swear to God I almost felt as naked before him as when I'd been wearing nothing but a towel.

"Well...*almost* everything I need," he added, and the words burned through me.

"Why did you need to measure the steam room?" I asked, ashamed at how rough my voice sounded.

"I'm retiling it. Starting next week, but I needed to get measurements for materials."

"Will it be usable while you're doing it?"

He shook his head, that silky black hair moving with him. I wondered if it would feel as soft as it looked. "No. I'll work during the nights, so the locker room will still be in use, but the steam room will be closed."

"For how long?"

He shrugged, looked at the figures he'd written down. "At least two weeks. Maybe longer. Depends how many hours I can put in on it each night."

"Oh," I said, disappointed. I really loved that steam room.

"The sauna will still be available."

I'd used the sauna, on the other side of the locker room, twice. But once I'd discovered the steam room, it just wasn't the same.

"But it's not the same," Lucas said, echoing my thoughts.

"I'll survive," I said. I hoisted my backpack up higher. "Well...um...good to meet you. Andy's a great kid." He nodded at that. There was nothing left to say. And yet I couldn't leave.

"Where do you live?" he asked.

"In Creyts. It's by—"

"I know where it is," he said, a tiny bit defensively.

"So...okay..."

"You're going to walk there by yourself? Across campus? At this time of night?"

"Yes." I did it a few nights a week, when I'd swum late, and steamed even later. I even studied here at times, in one of the classrooms in the old women's IM building. "It's fine. I do it all the time."

"You shouldn't," he said, and moved from where he stood to come and stand beside me. He effortlessly took my backpack from me and slid it across one of his broad shoulders.

"It's perfectly safe," I said, following him now as he started moving on without me. "What are you doing?"

He turned around and looked at me. "I'm walking you home," he said, then turned and kept walking.

Luckily I caught up to him just in time to hear him say, "Kade. My last name is Kade. Lucas Kade."

Something in me moved, and I knew that name—*his name*—would stay with me forever.

We walked to my dorm in silence. At first it felt like awkward silence to me, but then it just became…comfortable. Or more like comfort*ing*.

I walk this campus in the late evenings a few nights a week. And I don't feel *unsafe*, but then again, I'd never felt quite as secure as I did now, with Lucas's tall, strong body beside me. And that slight sense of danger, the feeling that as composed and controlled as he seemed to carry himself, he could unleash that big body with immense power at any time.

I admit it, I thought about all that strength and power unleashed on me. In a good way.

We passed people, most of whom I didn't know. Bribury was a small school, and you eventually knew a good portion of the student body, but I was a freshman, and had only been here a month. If I didn't have class with them, or they didn't live on my floor, I probably didn't know them.

The guys we passed looked at Lucas with curiosity. Lucas didn't belong amongst the Bribury boys in their skinny jeans, knit beanies, and impossibly fashionable eyewear.

And Lucas made them all look like just that…boys.

The girls we passed looked at Lucas with something more than curiosity. Hunger. Who could blame them?

I certainly felt him next to me—felt that strong, big body so close—even though we never touched. Not even the brushing of arms, though I admit I did come close to faking a stumble so I could lean into him.

But we reached my dorm with no stumbles—faked or otherwise—and I turned to him. "Here we are," I said, like an idiot.

He nodded, looking up at the four-story building. I didn't want to leave him, but I couldn't think of anything else to say.

"Have you worked for Bribury long?" I asked.

"Don't," he said, turning to face me full on. "You don't need to do that with me."

"Do what?"

"The small talk. The stuff you're doing with all the guys you're meeting. 'What's your major?' and 'Where'd you go to prep?' Don't do that with me. I'm not like them."

There was an intensity in his stance, in his face, though it was too dark to see if it showed in his eyes. My guess is it did.

We were standing to the side, at the front of the dorm, out of the lights from the doorway. I liked being in the shadows with him, but I also liked looking at his face. Too much.

"What are you, then?" I asked. "If you're 'not one of them'?"

"I'm..." He leaned toward me, took a tiny step closer. Not touching, but God, so close. I couldn't smell him and I wanted to, wanted to know his scent. Then something stopped him. He moved no further. In fact, he took a step back. I almost cried out for him to come back even though it was mere inches. He ran a hand through that black hair, that too long, not trendy-long, but shaggy-long, gorgeous hair. "I'm..." he began again. But his voice had changed; there was almost resignation now. "I'm not what you need," he finished.

He turned and walked away from me.

THREE

◈

"SO, LIKE, Matt Damon in *Good Will Hunting* janitor, or, you know, just skeezy, leering-at-college-girls janitor?" my roommate Jane asked.

"The Matt Damon kind, for sure," I said. We were sitting on our beds, facing each other across the small room.

"So, secret genius and all that? Deeply, deeply misunderstood?"

I shrugged and pulled one of the decorative pillows my mom had bought for my room onto my lap, as if I needed protection. "Probably not secret genius." I thought about the awareness in Lucas's eyes, and what seemed like intelligence. But how the hell would I know that? "At least, I don't think so."

"But big, you said? And kind of brooding?"

"Jesus, Jane, he wasn't Heathcliff or anything." Was he?

Jane flipped onto her back and stretched her long arms over her head. We were the same height—on the tall side—but Jane had more curves than me. A fact we both hated. She was in leggings and a T-shirt, both hugging her body. She wore her chestnut hair in a chin-length bob, sometimes straightening it, sometimes letting her wild curls run free, as they did now.

We didn't know each other before we became roommates, but we'd known *about* each other our whole lives. Our fathers had been deeply entwined with each other when Jane and I were born. And perhaps were again, if my father's instructions on keeping an eye on Jane were any indication.

For the first week, we'd warily circled each other, knowing we'd been placed together by our fathers, neither of us knowing exactly why.

The second weekend here, we'd gone to a party, gotten a little drunk, and done True Confessions back in our room, where we both agreed to disregard any directives coming from our fathers about each other, and just relax. Be friends. Real friends.

Which was an easy promise for Jane to make—she'd been ignoring her father's directives for years. Had taken great pleasure in it lately, in fact.

Not quite so easy for me, though.

"Poor Lily," Jane said, teasing in her voice. "A campus full of respectable, father-approved guys, and you fall for a ne'er-do-well townie."

"I'm not 'falling for' anybody," I said quickly.

Jane glanced my way and made a half-snort sound, then turned back to stare up at the ceiling.

"And we don't know that he's a ne'er do well," I added. I wasn't even sure what a ne'er do well was—Jane was always throwing out terms like that—but I figured it wasn't good.

"Right. 'Cause all guys at his age, with the world open to them, become janitors." She had a point. "I wonder if it's some kind of community service or something. Was he wearing an orange jumpsuit?" Jane said, laughing now at her own wit, slight as it was.

I didn't bother telling her that he wore jeans and a black polo…and wore them *well*. Instead, I threw my pillow at her and said, "Oh, shut up, already." Which made her laugh all the more.

"What's going on?" Sydney, our suitemate, said as she walked through the door adjoining our rooms. She had a sweatshirt on, and smelled like she'd just come from the outdoors.

Sydney O'Brien would not have felt afraid walking across campus at night. Syd would kick anybody's ass at Bribury, faculty included.

"Our poor Lily has it bad for a townie," Jane said. I wished I had the pillow back, so I could throw it at her again. Harder this time.

A look of distaste crossed Sydney's face. Which was rich, since she was a townie herself, just a different town.

Sydney came from a rough section of Queens and was at Bribury on a scholarship. She and Jane bristled each other frequently, but there was also a grudging respect for each other.

I, of course, was the peacekeeper between them when needed.

"Seriously?" Sydney said, looking at me. She moved to my desk and sat down. "Please tell me Jane is full of shit." She turned to Jane and added, "As usual."

"Haha," Jane deadpanned. "Not this time. Beautiful Lily, who could have any guy she wants, is going to slum it with a hoodlum."

"I don't know which part of that sentence to take issue with first," I said. I looked at Sydney. "Basically, it's all bullshit."

Sydney studied me, and I didn't like it.

Jane and I had grown up in spotlights, and Jane in particular had become world-savvy early on. But Sydney had us both beat when it came to life.

Sydney had *lived*. Though she was careful not to tell us much about it. It was as if she was reinventing herself at Bribury, cutting all ties to her previous life.

Part of me wished I could do that too, and so I admired Sydney. But I also worried about her.

There was a…desperateness…about how badly she wanted to fit in. I'd watched her studying how Jane and I dressed and acted. It wasn't *Single White Female*. She didn't want to *be* us. But she didn't want to be herself, either.

"*All* bullshit, Lil? Really? Beautiful? Check. Can get any guy you want? Check." I opened my mouth to object, but Syd raised a hand to stop me. "Get over yourself. Just because you don't seem to want any of the guys we've met so far, doesn't mean you couldn't have any one of them if you so much as crooked a finger."

"That's not true," I said, but they both ignored me.

"So, that leaves 'ready to slum it with a hoodlum.' What do you say, Lil? Is it a check?" There was teasing in Syd's voice. I looked at her, ready to throw back some trash, but couldn't. I looked at Jane, who was also smiling, but her grin faded when she saw my face.

"Oh, shit," Syd said, her teasing voice now gone. "It is a check. Isn't it? You're ready to hop in bed…with a *townie*?" The distaste in her voice was obvious.

That was the thing about Sydney—she was a poor scholarship student, but in many ways was a bigger snob than Jane or I ever were.

"I…I just met him," I said. I'd hoped to have more conviction in my voice, but it came out on kind of a whisper.

"Oh dear God," Jane said in her overblown, put-upon way.

Jane and Syd weren't wrong. I was what is considered classically beautiful—not that I did anything to look this way, other than have good genes, apparently.

And at the parties we'd gone to since arriving, and dorm functions, the boys did gravitate my way early on.

But there was…something…about Jane that made people want to spin in her orbit. It must have been what attracted her father to her mother. Jane had *it*.

And Sydney, well, I don't know what Sydney did for guys before Bribury, but her vaguely interracial look (which, let's face it, stuck out on this mostly white campus and seemed at odds with her O'Brien surname) and her tough-as-nails street attitude seemed exotic to the prep-schooled, silver-spooned male population.

And, like me, neither of them had found a guy here yet who sparked any interest for them.

Lucas Kade.

Even thinking about him sent a shudder through me. One that my roommates easily deciphered.

"Jesus, Lily," Sydney said as she rose from the chair and made her way to the doorway and back to her room. "With all these rich pretty boys here?" She was past the door now, but I could still hear her as she said, "Sounds like someone's working out a little rebellion issue."

I looked over at Jane, who quirked a questioning brow at me.

"That's not it," I said, though I wasn't sure I believed myself.

"That's too bad," Jane said, and hoisted herself from the bed and made her way to the bathroom. "Because that would be over and done with fairly quickly, with no broken hearts."

She closed the door behind her and I was left with my thoughts. Startled to think that maybe Sydney was right.

And scared to death that Jane was more right than Syd.

At the next swim lesson, there was no Lucas. And no Andy's mother, either. Somebody had dropped him off, but I hadn't seen them.

The lesson went well. Andy seemed much better at putting his head in the water. And somebody had obviously been working with Jessica, because she was turning into a little fish.

I hoped that these kids had the opportunity to get to a pool after the lessons ended. It would be a shame for them to just start to become acclimated to the water, then not get in a pool again for years.

It was already too cool for outdoor swimming, and there were no lakes or public beaches in the town that I knew of. Maybe there was a Y or something.

I kept myself from asking Andy who had dropped him off, but I noticed he did look up into the observation area a few time with expectation in his eyes, only to be disappointed.

And yeah…so did I.

And I hate to admit it, but while the girls ran through the shower, I took a little extra time and ran a brush through my wet hair and took it out of its ponytail, even though I'd be heading right back to the pool to swim laps.

Unless I had a better offer.

But no. No Lucas to pick up Andy. Instead, Andy slowly

walked forward when a guy, who definitely wasn't Lucas, sauntered down the hallway. He was Lucas's age and almost as tall as him, but this guy didn't have the strength and width across the shoulders that Lucas did. Same longer hair, but this guy's was wavy and deep brown instead of Lucas's straight, jet-black hair. And this guy seemed like maybe he hadn't owned a comb for a couple of years, though he looked clean enough. He had on a jean jacket and jeans, with shockingly white Nikes. Like, maybe he'd come straight here from the shoe store, they were so white and unsullied.

"Scruffy" was the word that came to mind looking at him. Cute in an edgy way, but not with any of the sheer beauty of Lucas Kade.

"Ready, champ?" the guy asked Andy. Andy nodded and left my side.

Nobody had gone over any kind of protocol on pickup with me, and I had this momentary flash of Andy being abducted by some unknown thug.

But Andy seemed to be expecting said thug. Still…I put my hand on his little shoulder. "Do you know this guy?" I asked Andy.

Andy looked up at me with confusion. "Yeah. That's Stick." Like, I should totally know Stick.

Stick was looking me up and down, and I wished I hadn't taken any extra time with my appearance. The knowing grin that spread across his face said he knew whom I was expecting to show up for Andy.

"Lucas is tied up right now," he said. "I'm getting Andy for him. Right, kid?"

Andy nodded and moved away from me, to Stick's (Stick? Seriously?) side.

I probably should have asked more questions, taken Stick's license number down or something, but I didn't. I just let Andy go with Stick.

There were no questions from Stick to Andy about how it went, or what to work on. Stick was pulling his phone out and doing something on it as they walked away from me.

Andy had been the last kid to be picked up, so all the other parents and instructors were gone, or back in the locker room.

This wave of…panic…came over me, and I raced down the hall. "Just one second," I yelled, and Stick and Andy stopped and turned to me. "I…I forgot to give Andy his assignment for next week," I said, though I had already talked about it with Andy while we'd been waiting.

Stick made an impatient wave with his hand, then kept texting, while I pulled Andy to the side, away from Stick.

I knelt down to Andy's six-year-old size and said very quietly, "Andy, were you expecting Stick to pick you up? Did your mother tell you you'd be going home with him? Or was it a surprise?"

"No. My mom didn't tell me Stick would be here," he said, and I felt another wave of panic. Crap, what the hell was I supposed to do now? Call the cops? Demand we all wait until Andy's mom could be notified?

A tiny bit of irritation crept in that I was being put in this position. I was a college freshman, alone for the first time. I was supposed to be the irresponsible one, out whooping it up.

And here I was wondering if I was caught up in a child abduction case.

"Lucas told me Stick would pick me up," Andy said. "Not my mom. My mom is…she's…gone away."

I didn't know what that meant in this kid's vernacular. Heaven? Prison? With the kind of life these kids lived, it could be either.

"But she's coming back," he added with vehemence. "She's coming back," he said more quietly, as if convincing himself.

"I'm sure she is," I said, though I wasn't sure at all. "So, Lucas told you Stick would be picking you up? You're sure?" He nodded, his wet hair sticking up in the back. I used my hand to tame the wild spot at the back of his head. "Okay, then, let's get you back to Stick."

Andy didn't seem to remember that I had said I wanted to

give him instructions, and Stick was still texting away. "All set," I said to Stick as Andy started leading the way. Stick started following Andy, then turned back and looked over his shoulder at me.

"Thanks, Lily," Stick said, then continued to follow Andy down the hall.

"No problem," I said, though they were now beyond hearing range.

I turned back toward the locker room. As I was walking I realized that neither I nor Andy had mentioned my name to Stick, and yet he knew it.

That thought sent a small, sick thrill through me.

FOUR

I SWAM hard, cutting through the water like it was silk, feeling my muscles stretch and burn, but in a good way.

And I took a long time in the steam room, savoring every moment, knowing it might be the last time I used it for several weeks.

Then I left the room. Okay, yes, I wrapped my towel very loosely around me. And yes, there were some strategic parts that I let the towel…*accidentally*…uncover. I left the room and turned to find…not Lucas. But somebody else.

"Jane? What are you doing here?"

She shrugged, like she hung out in locker rooms all the time, when I was willing to bet good money Jane had found a way to ace gym in high school without ever once seeing the inside of a locker room.

"I was on this side of campus and thought you might want to walk home together."

I eyed her suspiciously. "What were you doing on this side of campus at night?" I made my way to my row and down to my locker, throwing my wet suit onto the bench in front of it.

Jane sat on the bench a few lockers down, looking around, almost in fascination. (Yeah, this girl had never been in a locker room, for sure.)

"Um…I was…" Then she shrugged, giving up all pretenses. "So, is he here? Is he still in the steam room, totally wiped out from all the sweaty sex?"

"Yeah, 'walk home together' my ass."

She gave me one of her "so sue me" sigh and shoulder lift combinations, which I had come to know very well in the past month.

"He's not here. Didn't show at all. For Andy," I added, but Jane's smirk proved I didn't fool her.

Funny, I had resented her my whole life, without even knowing her. I was prepared to dislike her on sight…and I did. But a month later, I could read her like a book, as much as anyone could ever read Jane.

She read me much better. But then, I was pretty much an open book, whereas Jane had lots of chapters written in foreign languages, where you might make out a word or two, but the whole was confusing.

"Well, shit. I came all the way over here for nothing. I thought even if I didn't get a glimpse of Mr. Trouble, I'd at least get to see your afterglow."

"Nope. Sorry to disappoint."

Jane did stuff on her phone while I showered and changed. I didn't bother drying my long hair, just toweled it well and brushed it out. It wasn't cold enough yet to freeze it on the walk across campus. Plus, I had one of the ubiquitous beanies to wear if I needed it.

"It's kind of creepy in here, so deserted," Jane said as I packed up my backpack and we made our way to the door. I threw my towels in the large hamper as we passed it, and I thought of Lucas collecting random towels the last time I was here.

"Deserted, yes, but I don't think in a creepy way. More of a peaceful way," I said as we made our way out of the locker room, past the empty classrooms where I sometimes studied.

But there would be no studying tonight. It was Thursday, and Jane, Syd, and I only had one class on Fridays, and it wasn't until eleven. In fact, it was the only class we shared—a Humanities class taught by a visiting instructor.

So, on Thursday nights we got made up—using much effort to create a totally effortless look—and went to some party or another.

"And you're allowed to swim alone like that? With no one around? Seems like a big liability issue."

Jane's father—or sperm donor, as she called him—had made a mint in lawsuits before entering the political world. Much as Jane would hate hearing it, she had a brain much like her famous father. She was scary smart, never needing to study and, though it was early in the semester, it looked like she would four-point.

And, also like her father, there seemed to be a bit of a self-destructive streak in Jane.

Or so I had been told. And that was why I was here, with Jane, as her roommate.

"Technically, it's an open swim time, and there is someone on duty, but it's usually a guy and he uses the men's locker room—obviously. The women who swim here tend to be older—faculty, I guess—and they do it in the mornings. The locker room is pretty much mine after the swim lesson kids leave."

We walked out of the building and turned toward our dorm. "I guess most students use the newer IM building. I hear that's packed all the time." I looked up at the older, women's intramural building, covered in—you guessed it—ivy. It was much smaller than the new building, and on an inconvenient side of campus, but it had great character, and it wasn't a bevy of "notice me" students pretending at working out. It had cred, this building.

As we neared the corner, a car pulled up beside us and the driver's window lowered.

"Hey, little girls, how about some candy," the driver said.

We didn't look in their direction, just kept walking, although Jane did flip them the bird over her shoulder.

The car crept along beside us and I heard, "Lily."

I knew that voice. Even after only meeting once, I knew how he said my name.

I turned, and Jane stopped with me. The driver was Stick,

and he was the one who'd made the candy comment, but Lucas was leaning over him from the passenger seat so that I could see him. Or so he could see me.

"Get in, we'll give you a ride."

"Umm, that's—"

"Thanks, that would be great," Jane said, grabbing my arm and heading around the car to the passenger side.

It was an older car, and, like, souped up or something, though I don't know much about cars. It was dark, but I could tell the car was candy-apple red and was lovingly polished. It was also a two-door and the kind you got into the back by folding the front seat forward. Lucas stepped out of the car, held the door, and pressed the seat up, motioning me into the back. I climbed in, waiting for Jane to climb in next to me. Lucas held his hand out for Jane. "Hey, I'm Lucas Kade."

"Jane Winters. Lily's roommate." They shook hands, and I waited for Lucas to feel the spark, the fire, that seemed to emanate from Jane. But he held on to her hand and steered her to the front, then climbed into the back seat with me.

"Help Stick navigate, will you, Jane?" Lucas said as he pulled the front seat back into position. "Stick, Jane. Jane, Stick. Hey, Stick and Jane," Lucas said, and I smiled.

Stick and Jane did not. Jane gave Stick her "don't even think about it" look and Stick shot back a "you wish" glare.

Lucas grinned and sat back in the seat next to me.

Jane was obviously taking one for the team, and being an excellent wingwoman, because the way she looked at Stick—and she looked him completely up and down—said she'd rather be anywhere than next to him in a car that he was driving.

"Our dorm is the other way," Jane said when Stick took a left at the next corner, taking us away from campus and into Schoolport proper.

"Who said we were heading to your dorm?" Stick said, though he didn't look at her.

I could hear—*feel*—Jane's sigh, but I didn't care. Because I could also feel Lucas's presence next to me.

"Hey," he said in nearly a whisper.

"Hi," I whispered back, then ducked my head, embarrassed by my breathlessness. There was no disguising my desire from my voice.

I felt his finger on my chin, lifting my face, tilting it toward his. I looked up, met his brown eyes.

"Hi," he said, more firmly this time, and with such a soft, sweet smile that I felt it shimmer all the way through me.

"Hi," I said, more sure of myself this time. I was not alone in this. He felt it too.

"Do you need to get back to your dorm?" he asked.

I glanced at Jane's back and saw just the tiniest of headshakes from her, though she didn't say a word.

I'd owe her big time for tonight—a price I was more than willing to pay.

"No. We don't need to get right home," I said, Lucas's finger still on my chin. He nodded, then took his hand away, but not before he gently placed the finger on my bottom lip.

"Good," he said softly. Then, more loudly, "Stick, let's take a drive to the west side. I'm looking for some inspiration."

"You got it," Stick said, and roared the engine as we headed to the other side of Schoolport.

And I wondered why Lucas needed to be inspired.

And I hated to admit it, but I desperately wanted to be part of that inspiration.

FIVE

❖

WE DROVE for a while, past campus, past the nice area of downtown (small as it was), through the sketchy area of downtown (bigger), and to the downright scary area of the small city.

"God, this town is a total shithole," Jane remarked. She said the exact same words my father had told me when he'd dropped me off: "Stay on campus, Lily. This town is a shithole."

There was the same amount of judgment in both their voices.

"Well, not all of us were born with silver spoons," Stick said to Jane.

"Only half of a silver spoon. And it doesn't make the town any less of a shithole…asshole. What kind of car is this, anyway? I feel like I'm in a bad '70s cop show."

"This is a 1970 Dodge Charger," Stick said with obvious pride. "Restored to its original glory. An American classic."

"Yeah, a classic, all right…classic case of bad taste in cars."

And they were off. The verbal volleys flying fast and furiously between them. I'd heard Jane reduce guys to stammering idiots with her quick acid tongue, but Stick gave it right back to Jane.

Lucas smiled listening to them. "Fun with Stick and Jane," he said quietly to me. I returned his smile, stunned by the brilliance of his, the absolute transforming power of his smile, from broody tough guy to—dare I say—sweet.

"You have the most gorgeous smile," he whispered.

Jane and Stick were still talking up front, but their banter became white noise, and I felt the cocooning power of being alone with Lucas in Stick's back seat.

"I was just thinking the same thing about you," I said, then wished I hadn't. I grimaced at my stupidity.

"Don't," he said. "Don't ever regret telling me the truth." His voice was serious, the smile faded.

"I won't," I said, meaning it. Somehow I knew I could tell Lucas anything and he wouldn't think I was a clueless freshman.

"How old are you?" I asked. I knew he was older than me, but I didn't know by how much.

"Twenty-one. You?"

"Eighteen." He sighed what sounded like relief. "Almost nineteen," I added. "I was old for my class." I didn't add that my father wanted me to be in the same graduating year as Jane, so, even though I technically could have started school a year earlier, he'd waited. Never mind that we weren't even in the same school district that Jane's mom lived in.

My father—the puppet master even all those years ago. Did he really see this happening—Jane and I being roommates—so far in advance? My bet was yes.

"So, you can buy for us," Jane said from the front seat, and I realized that though I had tuned them out, she had not done the same to Lucas and me.

"We can," Stick said. "You ladies want to get wasted?"

"No," I said at the same time Jane said, "Yes."

Seconds later, Stick pulled up in front of a liquor store—a very shady-looking liquor store—and hopped out, leaving the car running.

Jane turned and looked at me, then at Lucas. Really looking him over, but not in a come-on kind of way. Jane and I had our issues, but she had a streak of loyalty in her that ran deep.

We'd only been roommates a week, and Jane had locked horns with Syd almost that entire time, when Jane and I overheard a couple of girls talking trash about Syd behind her back.

Jane called them out, intimidated the crap out of them.

When I asked Jane about it later, she just shrugged and said, "*I can tell Syd she dresses like a poser, but those two bitches better steer clear.*" I just shook my head at her logic. "Lily," she said, "she's ours. Syd, that is. And we take care of our own." To her, it was as simple as that.

"You're right," she said now as she turned from Lucas back to me. "Totally smoking hot." She turned back in her seat, facing the front, smirking at the position she'd put me in. "Too bad his friend is such a troll."

Lucas turned to me with a grin, and quirked a brow.

"I didn't say that," I said. Jane did a fake choke/cough/"bullshit" from the front. Lucas just smiled wider.

And moved closer to the middle of the seat. He patted the space between us and I moved closer to him. I was so drawn to him, I wanted to crawl right onto his lap, but I stopped myself. But the hungry look in his eye told me he wouldn't mind if I did.

So caught up in being close to Lucas, I started when Stick opened the car, handed a brown paper bag to Jane, and got in.

He roared off while Jane dug into the bag.

She pulled two beers out and handed them over the seat to us. Lucas took them both, twisted the lids, and handed one to me.

"Rolling Rock?" Jane said. "Seriously? They didn't have Sam Adams, or an IPA or something?"

"Big beer connoisseur at eighteen, are ya?" Stick said.

"I've had a few," Jane said, using the haughty voice she'd first used with me. For about a day.

"Nothing wrong with good old Rolling Rock," Stick said, taking the bottle Jane handed him and taking a large gulp. "Besides, it's about half the price of that fancy piss."

"I would have paid," Jane said.

The car slowed at a red light and Stick looked at Jane. "Let's get this straight right now. I don't take money from Bribury Basics. Got it?"

I waited for Jane's come back, but she just stared at Stick for a second. "Whatever," she finally said, and took a drink from her own beer.

Stick took another gulp and let out a large burp as the light turned to green and we rolled farther away from campus to the other side of town.

"Oh, that's attractive," Jane said to Stick's belch.

"Like I give a shit what you think."

"You owe me, Lily," Jane said.

We rode in silence until Jane asked, "Just why do townies call us Bribury Basics, anyway?"

"You really want to know?" Stick said, taking a glance at Jane.

"I asked, didn't I?"

I stiffened, waiting. I had a feeling we wouldn't want to hear this.

"You're all the same. You're all lemmings. Basic North Face jacket. Basic Uggs. Basic leggings or designer jeans. Basic long, straight hair. Nothing original, nothing unique, nothing…" He let the rest of his description fade away as he looked Jane over once again. Not one thing on Stick's list held true for Jane.

She was wearing this cool vintage Nehru jacket that I'd coveted the moment I saw her hang it in her closet. Though I'd probably never wear it even if I'd owned it. She also had on an older type of pants called painter's pants. I have no idea where she found them, but they were boxy and baggy and hung off her curves in a very flattering way. A filmy print peasant blouse under the jacket, and old-style white Chuck Taylors (not the cute new colored ones) on her feet. Shortish, chin-length hair was tucked behind her ears, trying to tame the wild curls.

She raised a brow at Stick, daring him to eat his words.

"Same basic Bimmer or Audi in the parking lot." Jane opened her mouth to argue, but Stick quickly finished with, "*When* you're allowed to have cars in the parking lot, second semester."

"Oh, so, so wrong, on all counts." Jane said what was obvious to all of us in the car, even those who had only met Jane tonight.

"Same basic Daddy's Little Princess," Stick said, trying to make a last throw onto the dartboard of Jane.

A bark of laughter came from Jane, sounding harsh, even for her. "Strike three, asshole. And you are *ouuuuut*."

Yes, the Bribury Basic label would never apply to Jane. And in a weird way, it was too bad, because Jane, on some level, did not want to stick out. Did not want to draw attention to herself. She would have loved to blend in, be a Basic in a sea of Bribury Basics.

But it just wasn't in her to do so. And I think that killed her. It reminded her that maybe she was in fact her mother's daughter. And that probably killed her even more.

But me? I looked down at myself. North Face jacket. Leggings. Uggs. Long, straight hair (though up right now because it was still wet).

I definitely fit the mold on the outside. But what was more, I *knew* I adhered to what Stick was really saying—there was no substance. I had followed the trends in high school. I was following them here at Bribury. I didn't want to stand out, not in a "what the hell is she wearing?" way, and knew enough to know how not to.

And the car? Well, a sleek blue Audi RS4 had been promised to me, as long as Jane stayed out of trouble our entire freshman year. Or at least didn't get caught or end up on YouTube or something.

It was naturally assumed that I would not do any of those things.

As for the Daddy's Little Princess? It galled me, but yeah, I was. At least in comparison to my older sister Alexis, who was what passed in our family for a wild child, though in reality, she wasn't much of one. And my younger brother Gray, who was beginning to bristle at my father's grooming of his future.

Although I hated that it mattered, it was important to me to be in my father's good graces, to have him…notice me, I guess.

Even if it was as a pawn in whatever game he was playing with Jane's father.

Lucas was looking over at me. Of course he'd known I was

the embodiment of the "lemming" Stick had described.

"Stick's full of shit," Lucas said softly.

"No I'm not. They're so—"

"Stick's full of shit," Lucas said again, loudly, firmly.

Stick finally got it. Perhaps because he had Jane sitting next to him, visually negating everything he was saying. "Ah, sorry, Lily. I didn't mean..." He couldn't finish. It was a lie. He had meant it. And what's more, he was absolutely right.

We all drank our beer and Stick drove us to a deserted-looking area. He turned the car so we were parallel to a long cement wall that was covered in graffiti. He put the car in park and cut the engine.

"Jane, would you please open your door and let me out?" Lucas asked.

Jane looked around at the desolate area, but did as Lucas asked, leaning forward in her seat so the back could go up. Lucas got out then held his hand out to me. "Come on," he said.

I took his hand. It was big and cold from holding his beer. I wiggled my way out of the car.

Jane lowered the seat and looked like she wanted to get out. Stick placed a hand on her arm. "Let's stay here and make a dent on this beer," he said. She looked up at me, silently asking me if I was okay being alone with Lucas.

I nodded and gave her a look—was she okay being alone with Stick? She gave a long-suffering sigh and nodded.

Yeah, I would owe her big. I saw a month of doing her laundry in my future.

Lucas shut the door behind me, keeping hold of my hand. I trailed behind him as he rounded the hood of the car and took the keys from Stick, who handed them to Lucas through the window, which he then rolled back up.

We went around to the back of the car and Lucas unlocked the trunk. He had to let go of my hand to rummage around. "Umm, you might want to not look in here," Lucas said. Which, of course, made me want to look in the trunk.

"Dead body?" I said, then wished I hadn't. Let's face it, I didn't know anything about Lucas Kade other than he had a brother named Andy Bell and he was going to be retiling my beloved steam room. And Stick? Well, for all I knew, there *could* be a dead body in Stick's trunk.

I turned away, looking at the wall that ran along what appeared to be some kind of freeway barrier. From the sounds coming from the other side, that was exactly where we were—on the other side of the freeway.

Which meant I was a long way from my safe, quiet dorm room.

I could hear metal shifting and clanging as Lucas searched for whatever he was looking for. I guessed I should be scared that he was going to come at me with duct tape and handcuffs, but I wasn't.

The trunk slammed and I jumped. "It's okay," Lucas whispered as he came up behind me. "Sorry to startle you."

"You didn't," I lied.

"Come here," he said, motioning me to join him along the side of the car. We leaned against the metal just past the back seat window, and Lucas set something on the roof. It was a spotlight, I discovered when he flipped the switch, illuminating a very large section of the wall.

"What are we looking for?" I asked.

"Not for. At," he said, leaning against the car. I leaned next to him and he put his arm on the car behind me, so that his shoulder brushed mine and his forearm was against my back.

I longed to snuggle into his side but I wasn't ready to make that move.

"What are we looking *at*?"

"The art."

"The graffiti?"

He shrugged, and I felt it along my shoulder. "I think of it as art. Some of these guys—these taggers—are some of the best artists I've seen."

I looked—really looked—at the wall again. He was right. Amidst the chaos were some really stellar works of art. Some Warhol-inspired sections. An area that had an awesome rendering of the president. Orioles' and Ravens' logos and stuff like that. And a bunch of small areas with just really cool designs and colors.

But my eyes kept getting distracted by the nonsense of penises and boobs, harshly done with black spray paint. "How can you focus on the good stuff through all of the crap?"

"Ah, Lily," he said, taking a drink from his beer. His hand moved from the car up my back to curve around my shoulder. "That's the secret of life, isn't it? Focusing on the art?"

"And ignoring the penises and boobs?" I teased.

He chuckled. It was a nice sound, one I hadn't heard before. And from his startled look, maybe one he didn't make very often.

"Well, you don't want to *totally* ignore boobs and penises," he said. "They certainly have their place." He gave a pointed look to my chest.

He pulled me closer to him and I burrowed into his side, a place I'd wanted to be since he'd climbed into the back seat with me.

Hell, a place I'd wanted to be since I saw him in the spectator area at the pool as I gave lessons to his little brother.

His hand rubbed my shoulder then moved to my neck, and he lightly grasped my nape. Warm and strong, his hand began to slowly move up and down on the back of my neck, his thumb gently stroking down the side. God, it felt so good. And so much *more* than I'd ever felt with any boy.

Maybe because Lucas wasn't a boy. And certainly not one of the brown-nosers who just wanted to date me to get in good with my father. Or who were afraid of my father.

"Do you know who my father is?" I asked Lucas.

He looked startled. "No. I don't think so."

"Grayson Spaulding?"

He shook his head. "Nope. Should I?"

I wrapped my arms around him, burrowing deeper, laying my

head against his broad chest. "No. You shouldn't. Never mind."

He didn't say anything further, just held me tighter. His hand slid from my neck into my messy bun.

"God, I can't wait to see your hair down when it's dry."

I thought about it. He'd only seen me with my hair in a bun in the pool, or after the steam room when it was soaking wet. When loose, my hair is down to my waist and is midnight black, just like Lucas's. But with some natural wave, not poker-straight like his.

"It's almost dry," I said, and took my arms from around Lucas to start pulling out the tie that held up my bun.

He stepped away from me, away from the car, to face me. He watched my face as I took out the bun, focused on my lips as I shook out my nearly dry hair. I fingered through the long tresses, pulling out snarls, while I focused on Lucas's hot gaze.

I bent over at the waist then came up quickly, tossing my hair back, like I was a stripper or something. I leaned back against the car, putting my hands on it behind me.

"God damn," he whispered, not getting it all out before his hands were on my face and his mouth was on mine.

He smelled like the freshly laundered cotton of his hoodie and a little of…car, I guess. I tasted the beer on his lips, then his tongue swept into my mouth and I stopped thinking about what Lucas Kade tasted like and just kissed him back.

Our tongues danced and played and he tilted his mouth for a better angle, taking the kiss even deeper. I took my hands from the cold metal of the car and placed them on the warm cotton of Lucas's hoodie. I felt the muscles in his chest flex at my touch, but I just wanted to taste him. My entire being focused on the kiss, his mouth on mine, demanding, conquering, yet giving as well. I moaned into his mouth as he nipped my lower lip.

"Jesus, Lily," he said, and took my mouth again. I wrapped my arms around his neck and he stepped closer to me, leaned into me. My fleece pulled up and I could feel the denim of his jeans on my bare belly.

He pushed his hips into me and I felt his erection. I shifted my legs, opening my stance so he could get closer. Closer. It couldn't be close enough. I grabbed on to his hair, running my fingers through it, clutching his neck. I rubbed up against him like a cat in heat. "Lucas," I whispered against his mouth, then ran my tongue along his full lips.

"I know, baby," he said. Like he knew how crazy this was, going at it against a car when I barely knew him. He pulled away and put his hands along my face, forcing me to look at him.

I felt dazed, drugged, and it seemed like he did too.

"I know," he repeated, echoing my thoughts. "But I can't…" He didn't say more, just kissed me again. Sweetly at first, as if he didn't want to scare me. Even though my feelings for him—so strong, so fast—were scaring the crap out of me. I kissed him back, trying to let him know I was okay. He figured it out, taking the kiss deeper again, grinding his erection into me as I shifted closer, meeting him.

"Dude, we gotta go," Stick said from his window, which I hadn't even heard being rolled down, as induced in my Lucas fog as I was.

"What?" Lucas said, pulling away from me. He was in as much of a haze as I was, looking at me as if I'd said the words.

"Dude. Lucas. We've got to go, man," Stick said, causing Lucas to look from me to his friend.

A look passed between them. Lucas nodded. In a flash he'd turned off the spotlight, put it back in the trunk, and herded me around the car to where Jane let us in.

We sped away and back through town.

"Sorry to do that to you, man, but I got a call," Stick said, meeting Lucas's eyes in the rearview mirror.

"It's okay," Lucas said. The look he gave me said it was anything but okay—it was full of regret and unfinished business.

He put his arm around me, and I again resisted the urge to crawl onto his lap. But this time, I did move very close, and laid a hand across his chest.

IN TOO DEEP ⁘ 39

His hand played in my hair, occasionally massaging my neck and scalp. It felt incredible.

"Why did we go there?" I asked. He leaned into my neck, nuzzling.

"Wasn't it obvious?"

"No. I mean, why *there*? How was that place inspiration?"

He took a drink from his beer, draining it. "I like looking at the colors the taggers are using. Some of the designs. It gives me ideas for tiling jobs."

"You mean you're going to do a tile mosaic of the president in my steam room?"

He smiled, placed a soft, warm kiss on my lips, then shook his head. "Nah. I'm thinking more like penises and boobs."

I laughed, reveling in our private joke. Jane and Stick had been silent since we'd gotten back in the car. From the stiff set of Jane's shoulders, I guessed I was looking at more like *two* months of doing her laundry.

As we got back to the small, swanky area of town, the car slowed down along a row of parked cars. A fancy French restaurant was on one side, a trendy fusion place on the other. Valets were running cars for both places, as the street had no parking. Diners got out of expensive cars and headed into the restaurants.

I hadn't known about this small pocket of town, and figured it'd be about the only area my parents would deign to go to when they'd come to pick me up for break.

Stick pulled the car over onto a side street just past the row of restaurants. In a moment, a valet came over to Stick's window.

I was confused. Were we going to one of these places to eat? Stick and Lucas did not seem the valet-parking kind of guys. More like they'd be the valets themselves.

But no, the valet handed Stick something that I couldn't make out, looking at Jane first, then into the back seat. "Hey, Lucas," he said. Lucas didn't say a word, just gave a slight chin raise to the guy.

"Hour and a half, max," the valet said to Stick.

"Got it," Stick said. The valet stepped away and returned around the block to the restaurants.

"What do you think, Lucas?" Stick said. "Getting any more inspiration?"

"No inspiration here," Lucas said, his voice sure, and with just a touch of steel in it. "Move on, Stick."

"You never know, you might find something that strikes you," Stick said as he put the car in gear and drove.

I cuddled into Lucas, but his hand in my hair had gone still.

"Nope. Not here. Let's just take Lily and Jane home," he said.

The drive home was quiet until just as we were reaching the dorm and Lucas asked me for my phone. Jane got out of the parked car as I handed my phone over to Lucas and he punched in some numbers as he got out and let me past him. His phone rang and he disconnected the call he made to himself.

"There," he said, handing the phone back to me. "Now we have each other's numbers." He looked like he wanted to kiss me, but he just got back into the car and Stick sped off.

"Oh, he's got your number, all right," Jane said as she turned and walked into the dorm.

I stood and watched until I couldn't see the car lights anymore.

SIX

❖

"**YEAH, I'M** thinking laundry for two months," Jane predictably said the next day when we were in our one shared class—Intro to Creative Writing.

She'd been blessedly quiet after Lucas and Stick dropped us off at the dorm. Although it helped that she'd gotten a phone call from her father. They'd argued, as usual, while I'd gotten ready for bed. And when she'd hung up, she'd been too preoccupied to grill me about Lucas.

I'd woken up earlier than her this morning and dressed quietly, not even showering, and left the room before she woke.

But the instructor was late, also as usual, and it was obvious that Jane had filled Syd in during their walk to class, because they'd sat on either side of me and given me "okay, spill" looks the moment they sat down.

"Where is Montrose? You'd think an eleven o'clock class wouldn't be too taxing to get up for. I mean, we usually party on Thursday nights and we make it on time," I said, trying to deflect.

"Yes, that's right, we *usually* party on Thursday nights. But that's not what we did last night, is it?" Jane said.

I didn't answer. Syd piped in with, "Well, I did. I wasn't going to stay home just because you dragged Jane into your ghetto love fest." She was teasing, even nudged me, but the words rang true. That area with the graffiti wall was about as ghetto as you could get.

"Hardly a love fest," was my weak answer.

"Please. I didn't turn around—who needs to see gorgeous people making out when I'm stuck with a troll loser—but I could feel the car rockin'," Jane said.

Deflecting again, I said, "That's the second time you've called Stick a troll. I think he's kind of cute. In a scruffy kind of way."

She shrugged. "Meanwhile, you were in the back seat with an Adonis."

"Okay. Laundry for two months," I said, verbally conceding to what I'd already conceded to in my head the night before.

Jane looked smug and turned her attention to her phone. Syd nudged me again. "Jane gave me most of the details on the way here. Just how far did it go on the trunk of the car?" It wasn't a plea for juicy details—which we all normally shared after any kind of hookup. There was concern in Syd's voice.

"Not very," I said truthfully. But although it was true, we hadn't gone very far, it wasn't exactly the *whole* truth. Which was… although it was just kissing, I felt a much deeper connection to Lucas in even this short time, than I'd ever felt with any other guy. "Just kissing. A tiny bit of grinding." Syd nodded, waiting for me to go on. I shrugged. "That's it. It was all pretty innocent."

She gave me a cool look. "I don't know. This guy seems out of your world, Lily. Definitely not what you're used to in guys."

"Isn't that the whole point of college? To find new worlds?"

"You're not freakin' Columbus," Jane muttered from my other side, but continued to keep her eyes glued to her phone, her fingers tapping furiously.

"Yes," Syd said. "That is what college is about. But *good* new worlds. Challenging new worlds. Worlds that help you grow. This…" She waved her hand absently at me. "This is not the kind of new worlds you should be exploring. That world will only hold you back." She said the last bit softly, and I knew she was speaking from experience.

I laid a hand on her arm, gave her a squeeze, then took it away. Neither Syd nor Jane were big on touching. "I'm not planning on immersing myself in Lucas's world. Hell, I don't even know what his world is. We did meet on campus."

"Because he's a *janitor*," Syd said, sounding more like Jane.

A snort from Jane confirmed that comparison.

"Actually, I think he's more than that. I think he does… like…specialty tiling or something."

Another snort from Jane. "And that's supposed to make it better."

Syd was opening her mouth, and I put my hand out to stop her. "Look. Both of you," I said, and waited until Jane's fingers stilled and she looked my way. "I appreciate the concern. But… and I say this with love…back the hell off."

Jane smiled, returned to her phone, and said softly, "Well, well, Lily *does* have a backbone."

I should have been pissed at what she said, but I was, in a small way, kind of proud of it. And, in a larger way, I kind of agreed.

Syd looked like she wanted to say something, but just gave me a nod and turned to her laptop.

"Morning, all," William Montrose said as he entered the small classroom. No explanation or apology for being late. And just barely under the wire of the time when we could have called "no class" and left.

"Nice of you to show up," Jane muttered under her breath, as she put her phone away and pulled out her laptop.

"Always nice to see you too, Miss Winters," he replied as he dumped a messenger bag on the desk next to the lectern, then sat on the front of the desk, facing the small class. "Always a pleasure," he drawled in Jane's direction, giving her a "yeah, I heard you, bitch," look, which Jane laughed at.

I don't know what she was like in other classes, but Jane liked to yank Montrose's chain, and openly flirted with him. "I'd climb him like a tree in a second," she'd said after our first day of the Monday-Wednesday-Friday class.

He gave it right back to Jane, but never reciprocated in the flirting. Which just made her try all the harder. He was a good-looking guy, probably in his late twenties. Apparently he'd been some kind of big deal a few years back when he'd published a book that was at the time considered his generation's *On The Road*. I don't think he'd done much since. And if he was down to guest teaching Intro to Creative Writing at Bribury College, then my guess was his literary star had fallen hard.

"So. Let's talk about omniscient point of view, shall we?" he said, launching into a discussion I barely heard. I'd have to look at Jane's or Syd's notes later, because as much as Montrose was older-man eye candy, my mind could not stay on him today.

No, my mind was firmly back in front of that tagged-up wall, with my hands in Lucas's hair and his hips grinding into mine.

I googled him. Of course I googled him. But there wasn't much. Apparently he'd been a big deal football player in high school (which explained the rockin' bod and skyscraper height). He'd even gone to USC on a scholarship, but apparently had torn something in his shoulder, or elbow, and couldn't catch the ball anymore. Which, as a wide receiver, was pretty much his entire job. Obviously he wasn't still at USC. So he had come back east, back home. And was tiling Bribury's steam room.

There was a story there, for sure, but it didn't show up online.

He wasn't on Facebook, Twitter, Instagram, or any of the other social media sites. I even did a search for "Stick" in conjunction with Lucas Kade. Nada.

Then I googled myself to see what would show up, just in case, on the crazy off chance that Lucas would google me.

Not surprisingly, it was all stuff about my dad, where I would be mentioned in the last line, as part of his bio.

Yep, my entire online footprint was as an afterthought to my father's many political king-making coups. There were a few mentions of me winning swim meets. But that was it. So I would remain as much a mystery to Lucas as he was to me.

Except there wasn't much more to me.

And I knew there was much, much more to Lucas.

I waited until the last possible moment on Friday night to go out with Syd and Jane. Lucas hadn't called or texted and I didn't want to call him. I'd called guys before, and had nothing against it. But those were with guys whom I was sure wanted to hear from me. And although I knew Lucas was attracted to me—he couldn't hide that big erection while he was pressed up against me—I wasn't totally convinced he wanted to see me again so soon.

Or ever.

No. I knew he did. I knew he felt the bone-deep connection that I did. You just couldn't fake that. What I didn't know was if he'd act on it.

I'm not what you need.

He wasn't. I knew that. But I also knew that I'd be available the next time he called.

So we went out on Friday night. Jeff, one of the kids on the floor below us, had an older brother who lived just off campus in one of the few nice apartment complexes. The brother was having a party, and Jeff had been trying to get on Jane's good side from day one, so we were invited.

We partied. Jane drank too much beer and gave poor Jeff no encouragement whatsoever. That didn't keep him from hanging around her all night, feeding her beers and hoping.

Syd made a play for the older brother, who looked like he'd be stepping into daddy's law firm the moment he passed the bar.

Pretty, entitled rich boy. But basically an okay guy. Bribury was full of 'em. I'd grown up with them. But Syd hadn't. And you could tell she desperately wanted to be part of that. I could have told her it wasn't anything special.

The older brother wasn't biting at Syd's hook, so she left when Jane and I did. On the walk home, Jane pinballing between Syd and me, I kept an ear out for a louder, older car, but none came.

A text woke me up the next morning at nine.

You awake?

Lucas.

I snatched the phone off my pillow and texted back that I was. The phone was ringing seconds after the text went through.

"Morning," he said, his deep voice the best wake-up call ever.

"Hi," I said.

"Did my text wake you?"

"No," I said, though it had.

"Liar," he said, a chuckle in his voice.

I smiled. "It's okay. I'm glad you called."

"Late night last night?" he asked. It should have been a routine question for waking someone up at nine, but there was a hint of…just a smidge of…pissiness in his voice. And that pissiness made me tingle with excitement.

"Not too late," I said, not willing to let him off the hook quite yet.

"How late is not too late?"

"Well, since I didn't hear from you, I'm not sure you get to know."

There was silence, and I panicked that maybe I'd gone too far. But I held my ground—something I probably wouldn't have done before.

"You're right. I don't get to know." I waited. "Listen, I'm taking Andy swimming today. They have open swim time until two, and I can take him now that I'm a Bribury employee."

"That's nice," I said. "He'll love that." I was trying to figure out if he wanted tips on what Andy should be working on or what.

"Wanna come with us?"

"Swimming? With you and Andy?" I asked, surprised. "You mean as, like, his instructor or something?"

"No. Like…a…friend of mine who's just hanging out with us."

"Umm…" My mind was spinning with what this meant. Would he want me around Andy as Lucas's "friend" if he didn't want me in his life? At least as more than just a hookup against the side of a car?

"You don't have—" he said at the same time I said, "Yeah, I'd like that."

"Really?" he said. For the first time since I'd met him, there was uncertainty in Lucas's voice. It made me even hotter for him.

If that was possible.

"Really," I said softly, but firmly, trying to convey how much I wanted to see him in that one little word.

"I'm borrowing a car. I can pick you up."

"Why don't I meet you there? I can walk."

"Okay. Like, eleven?"

"Eleven is good. I'll meet you at the pool."

"See you then," he said.

"Okay," I said. Neither of us hung up. "Lucas?"

"Yeah?"

"I wasn't out that late," I said. "And I thought of you the whole time," I added, then quickly cut the call.

SEVEN

LUCAS KADE was even more impressive in board shorts. He had one tattoo circling a well-defined bicep. Stark and black, it wasn't barbed wire or a tribal symbol, but a chain of what looked like ivy. On the back of each arm was the number eight.

"Eighty-eight was my number when I played ball," he explained when he caught me looking.

And look I did. My God, what a body. Lean and long, but strongly muscled. His back bore the ink "Andy" very small across his shoulder blade, and I smiled as I saw the name ripple with muscle while Lucas lugged Andy around the shallow end.

"You're doing great, buddy," Lucas said. Andy, of course, was in heaven.

And yeah, so was I.

We played a game of Marco Polo close to the edge so Andy could keep a hand on it if he needed to. By the end of our session, he was leaping—albeit with his eyes open—away from the wall a few times to Polo Lucas and me.

"That's it for today, buddy," Lucas said when Freddy, who was picking up a shift as the lifeguard on duty, called the end to the open swim time. For the last hour we'd been the only ones in the pool. And for the last half-hour I'd swum laps while Lucas worked with Andy on putting his face in the water.

I swam to a corner of the shallow end, where the two brothers were.

"You're an awesome swimmer, Lily," Andy said.

"Thanks, Andy. Keep practicing and you'll be able to swim that long too."

Andy gave me a skeptical look, and it was the first time I saw a resemblance to Lucas. And, I have to say, it was a bit disconcerting.

"She's right. Keep at it, buddy, and you'll be swimming laps with Lily someday."

I noticed the skepticism left Andy's face when Lucas piped in. Serious case of hero worship going on there.

I knew Lucas was no hero, but the way he was with his little brother certainly made his stock rise with me.

And those rock-hard abs didn't hurt his stock, either.

We all moved to the ladder, and Andy scampered up first, then moved to the side of the pool where we'd laid out towels. He wrapped up in one and plunked down on the bench, watching as Freddy moved some of the unused lane markers on the other side of the pool.

I moved for the ladder next, but Lucas reached out and wrapped his hands around my waist, pulling me back into him.

"Is it wrong that I got super hard watching you swim?"

I laughed, then let out a sigh as I felt his bulge against my ass, right where he'd positioned me. "If your brother saw, then yes, it would be wrong."

"Good thing he's not opening his eyes under water yet," he said, his voice low and husky. My hands were on the metal rail to the ladder. I moved to release them, but a quiet "don't," from Lucas made me stop.

One of his hands moved up from my waist to cup a breast. I looked over at Andy, but he was at the wrong angle to see what was going on. Plus, he was still engrossed in whatever Freddy was doing.

"Freddy," I said softly, warning.

"He's busy. Besides, I've got your back. Literally."

And he did, leaning that strong chest against my back,

making me wish the racer back of my suit was completely gone.

I'd briefly contemplated wearing a bikini to swim today, but thought that might be trying too hard, when I'd always been in a proper swimsuit with Andy before.

But now. God, now I'd give anything to have less Lycra between Lucas and me.

I leaned back into him, keeping my arms on the bars, giving him access to…everything.

One hand continued to knead my breast, shaping, flicking across the nipple as I felt it tighten to a sensitive bud. His other hand slipped lower, right down the front of me. Right down to the core of me.

His finger teased the elastic of my suit along my inner thigh. I lifted one leg on the ladder, giving him better access, loving how dangerous it all felt, with Freddy on the other side of the room and Andy just a few yards away.

Loving how Lucas made me feel.

His long finger edged under the elastic, turned and sought. My hands wrapped tighter on the metals bars, wishing it was Lucas I was hanging on to as he teased my outer lips, brushed ever so lightly across my slit.

"Lily, are you going to have pizza with us? Lucas said if I put my head under water three times we can have pizza. And I did it." Andy got off the tile bench and made his way over to us, just as Lucas slipped his hands off my body.

I wanted to scream at Andy. To tell the poor kid to sit the hell back down so his brother could keep his glorious hands all over me. So that I could feel the cool glide of that searching finger deep inside me.

Instead, I rose up the ladder, the steel bars cold against my hot skin.

"I know you did," I said to Andy as I rose from the pool, the water sluicing down my trembling legs. "I saw. I think it was even more than three times." I had no idea—my eyes had been on Lucas's body when he'd been working with Andy—but I took a shot.

Andy's little face beamed, and I knew I'd shot correctly. "I did. Four times!"

"Wow, that's great, Andy," I said, making my way over to the bench, Andy trailing behind me. I grabbed a towel and another one to hand to Lucas. When I turned, he was still in the pool, his eyes firmly planted on my ass. Well, my front now.

I held the towel up to him, my eyes questioning why he was still in the pool. He gave a tiny shake to his head and then eye-pointed to what was undoubtedly a still very hard hard-on.

I was happy to confirm that you indeed could not see anything below the pool's edge from this angle. And also happy to confirm that I got Lucas as turned on as he got me.

Andy was between us with his back to me, so I rubbed my towel slowly across my breast, cupping it and stroking it more than drying my suit.

"You're not helping," Lucas said with a growl, but the heat in his eyes told me he enjoyed the show.

I was about to take it further—Lucas made me want to be bold, and I was not a bold girl by nature—when Andy turned back to me, causing me to pat myself dry with the towel like a normal person. Not like someone dying to have Lucas's hands all over them again. And soon.

"So, are you gonna have pizza with us?"

I looked past Andy to Lucas, to gauge how I should answer. Did he want me to have pizza with Andy and him? Or was I just helpful for the pool part of their guy day because I was Andy's instructor?

I waited, staring at Lucas, who stared back. I could see a hundred emotions playing across his gorgeous face, but I couldn't read them.

"It's a Saturday night, buddy," he finally said to Andy, though his eyes didn't leave mine. "Lily might have big plans. Might have another party to go to." There was that pissiness again, and it thrilled me.

Childish, I know. But I felt the same way. The thought of Lucas out at a party, no doubt with some girl—or two or three—trying to get with him, made me insane. It was an emotion I had no right to, no claim of any kind. And yet…I felt it.

And I knew Lucas felt it too.

"Am I invited for pizza?" I said quietly to Lucas. My chin raised in answer to his tone, challenging him.

"Yes," he said, deep and throaty, at the same time as Andy's sweet little voice said the same thing.

"Then I'd love to come," I said.

"I'd love to watch you…*come*," Lucas said, with an eighth-grade boy's maturity.

I should have rolled my eyes at the bad pun, and the pervy tone in his voice. Instead, I just looked back at him and mouthed, "You will."

Andy smiled and said, "Yay, Lily's coming," then plucked his towel from the bench and began haphazardly to dry himself off.

"Here, let me help," I said, sitting on the bench and motioning for Andy to stand in front of me, which he did.

I took his towel from him and began to dry him off, as I did with the little girls in my swim class when we went into the locker room.

"Probably no sense in doing this now," I said, though I continued to do so. "You're going to take a shower soon and get all wet again."

Andy shrugged his little shoulders, and only turned around and held his arms out from his sides so I could dry his back.

Lucas still watched us from the pool, I assumed still trying to gain control. I silently wished him luck with that, because I seemed to have lost all sense of control from the moment I saw Lucas Kade sitting on these very bleachers.

He rose from the water then. Instead of using the ladder as Andy and I had, he hoisted himself out with his arms onto the side of the pool deck.

God, those glorious arms, bulging and flexing with the

weight and effort. Water ran down his muscled chest. I longed to trail my tongue along the ridges and hard muscle that the moisture followed.

I took Andy's scrawny arms in the towel and gave them a quick drying, absently wondering if Lucas's magnificent build came more from his mother or father. If Andy would one day be as big and strong as his older half brother.

As Lucas walked over to us and grabbed his own towel, I tried to remember their mother. She'd brought Andy the first week of lessons but hadn't stayed to talk with me. The week after that, she had again quickly left as soon as Andy was out of the locker room, not waiting to speak with me about Andy's progress. I hadn't even gotten the girls out of the locker room before Andy was gone. Then this past week it had been Lucas, and then Stick, who had picked up Andy from his lesson.

My mind searched for an image of Andy and Lucas's mother, though I had only basically seen the back of her as she'd herded Andy down the hall.

Not that I expected she'd have the build of a college football star, but I seemed to remember her coloring was more like Lucas's—dark—as opposed to Andy's fair hair and skin.

"Okay, buddy, let's get going so Lily can go change," Lucas said, placing his hand on Andy's shoulder.

Andy seemed reluctant to leave the warm petting I was giving him with the towel, but when Lucas placed his hand on Andy's shoulder, the little boy melted into his brother's body, snaking a small arm up and around Lucas's back.

A place I couldn't wait to snake my hands around, too.

"Meet you in front of the locker rooms?" Lucas said, as we all started moving toward the locker room doors. I waved a goodbye to Freddy, who answered with a wave of his own.

"See you in a few," I said as I got to the women's door.

"Lily," Lucas said, and I turned to him. "Don't take too long. I can't wait to…have pizza." His hungry glance up and down my body told me he was going to be having much more than pizza this evening.

"I can't wait, either," I said as I ducked into the door.

I'd never said truer words.

EIGHT

"IS THIS your car?" I asked as we drove away from campus.

"No, it's Stick's. He's letting me borrow it for a while."

It was similar to the one we'd ridden in Thursday night—older, but restored with loving care—but this one was a shiny deep blue instead of candy-apple red.

"Is this a…what did Stick say the other night? A Charger?"

He shook his head, a smile on his face at my lack of car knowledge. "No. This is a 1972 Chevy Camaro. Vastly different."

It didn't look that different to me, other than the color. "How does Stick own so many cars? What does he do?"

Lucas took a quick look in the rearview mirror into the back seat at Andy, who was looking out the window, seemingly oblivious to Lucas and me.

"Stick is…self-employed," Lucas said to me in a tone that said I'd be smarter to just leave it at that. Which I did.

"Does he fix these cars up himself?"

Lucas nodded. "He's been a car nut for as long as I can remember. We'd be on the street playing ball, and Stick would be there, but instead of playing ball, he'd have his head under the hood of a car."

"Playing ball. Something you were pretty good at, right?"

He glanced over at me. "Yeah, I was pretty good. For about a minute."

"Then you got hurt," I said. It wasn't a question. I wanted

him to know I knew a little bit about him, even though there wasn't much to know—at least not online.

He looked in the rearview again as we came to a red light. A smile, so sweet and unplanned, crossed his face. I turned to see what had made Lucas smile. Andy's little strawberry-blond head was lolling against the car window, his seatbelt the only thing holding him upright. His eyes were drooping past half-mast, then flickering, in a valiant effort to try to stay awake. An effort he'd soon lose.

Lucas returned his attention to me—to my statement about him playing ball. He ran a hand across the back of his neck, under his shiny, wet black hair. He eased the car forward when the light turned green, careful not to roar like Stick had, so as not to wake Andy.

"Yeah, I guess it's time for that talk, isn't it?" he said, resignation in his voice.

I so didn't want to be something Lucas resigned himself to. "What talk?" I asked, though I thought I knew what he meant.

"The Life and Times of Lucas Kade," he said, a trace of bitterness creeping through in his voice. "Or, how an A-1 college recruit and NFL hopeful ended up tiling steam rooms in his shithole hometown."

Definite bitterness now.

"We don't have to if you don't want to," I said, though I was dying to hear his story. Dying to know everything I could about the man whose hands made my body sing with tension and arousal.

And yes, made my pulse beat faster and my heart clench when he looked at me with those piercing brown eyes.

"No, I'll tell you. It's only fair. Because Lily," he said, his voice dropping to a low and throaty—and oh-so-sexy—whisper. "I want to know everything about you. I want to hear every story. Touch every part of you." He looked at me then, and my blood raced through my veins at his promise. "And taste every inch of your body."

My breathing became heavy, my chest lifted and tightened. Lucas noticed, and when his eyes lifted to my face, I licked my lips and gave him a slight nod.

We both knew what I was agreeing to.

Because Andy was dead to the world, we decided to just go back to their place and order a pizza. I watched as Lucas sweetly carried a sleeping Andy from the car into a four-story apartment building. If I had my bearings—and I wasn't sure I did—we weren't too far from the graffiti wall part of town.

Their apartment was on the second floor. Lucas easily held Andy while pulling out keys and unlocking the apartment door. It looked like a practiced move, and again I racked my brain for memories of the elusive mother. Was Lucas responsible for Andy all the time?

The apartment was small, the main room not much larger than my dorm room. The furniture was old and shabby, but the place was super clean. A tiny kitchen with a table and three chairs was on one side. I could see three doors down the hallway, figuring two bedrooms and a bath.

Toys were strewn around the small place, mostly trucks. A large flat-screen TV was against one wall on a table that seemed too small for the large screen. Several items sat on the floor around the table, as if they'd been recently displaced by the large TV.

"I'm going to put him down, then order the pizza," Lucas quietly said as he walked down the hallway. He took Andy into the room farthest down the hall.

I dropped my backpack on the floor by the door and made my way to the couch, curling up in one of the corners. I pulled my North Face off and tossed it on the chair in the corner of the room. I noticed three large boxes tucked neatly behind the chair, out of the way. Yeah, it kind of seemed like maybe somebody with a big-ass TV had just plunked down into this little apartment.

Lucas was back out in a flash, a smile on his gorgeous face. "He is *out*," he said, "but I know that doesn't last long at this time of day. He's going to wake up starving in about an hour."

His eyes roamed over me. I'd put my North Face on over my leggings and tiny knit shirt in the locker room, so Lucas hadn't seen me without the bulky jacket until now. The way I was sitting had made the hem of my shirt ride up a bit, and his eyes zeroed in on the skin showing. I still had a tiny bit of tan left from lifeguarding at the country club last summer, though that was more on my face and arms, since I didn't wear a bikini often, even though it was technically allowed.

Lucas made his way over to me. He was about to sit next to me, then stopped. With a pained look on his face and a sigh, he pulled out his phone from his jeans pocket. "Let me just call and get the pizza. I'm serious, he's going to wake up starving. And Andy may seem like a sweet kid, but he turns into a whiny little shit when he's hungry."

I laughed. "Yeah, well, so do I." He'd been walking away from me, toward the kitchen area, but looked at me over his shoulder at that and smiled.

God, when he smiled at me I just wanted to peel all my clothes off and rub myself all over his big, strong body.

"Somehow I don't see you doing whiny," he said. He went to a drawer, opened it, and started rummaging around what looked to be delivery menus.

My phone vibrated in my jacket pocket and I reached for it on the chair—nothing was very far away in the small room. I pulled it out of my jacket and looked.

Syd and I going to a party later tonight. Will you be back? Jane had texted.

I looked at Lucas's back, how his broad shoulders tapered down to his waist and how his jeans fit so perfectly. And that ass. Good Lord, where to start on Lucas's ass?

No. Have fun, I texted back.

Lucas turned and walked back to me, a pizza menu in his hand. "What's up?" he said, motioning with his chin to the phone in my hand.

"Nothing," I said. "Just Jane checking in."

"Afraid you came to the dark side of town and disappeared?" He was teasing, but there was something a little serious in his voice. A little defensive, and I knew I'd need to be aware of, and careful of, Lucas's slight insecurity about where he came from.

Hey, we all had our shit to deal with. I knew I certainly did.

"No, not that. She just wanted to know if I wanted to go to a party with her and Syd—that's our suitemate—later." I had meant to show that Jane wasn't concerned about my safety, but I realized by the look on Lucas's face that I probably shouldn't have been so honest.

"*Do* you want to go to the party with them? 'Cause I can bring you home as soon as Andy wakes up. Hell, I can have Mrs. Jankowski come over and stay with Andy and I can take you home right now." He rattled this all off so quickly, I almost didn't grab his hand in time before he'd turned and walked away from me, presumably to make plans to take me home.

But I did grab his hand, and I held on tight. I even reached out with my other hand, holding his in a tight grip. "Wait. No. No, I don't want to go to the party. I want to stay here." He looked down as he stood over me. A thousand emotions played over his face.

I'm not what you need. His words to me that first night played over in my mind.

He was probably right, but right now I needed nothing as much as I needed Lucas Kade to want to be with me. To want to hug and kiss me. To want to do everything to my body that I wanted to do to his.

I tugged on his hand. "Lucas," I whispered. I leaned back into the corner of the couch, pulling him with me. He didn't resist, but he didn't fall on top of me, either. "I don't want to go to any party tonight. I just want to be with you."

He put a knee on the couch next to my hip. He held out his free hand in front of my phone, like he wanted me to hand it over to him. Did he want to check and make sure I wasn't lying?

Would he be that type of guy, always checking my phone? I could see that kind of possessiveness from Lucas, but not that kind of insecurity. But really, how well did I know him?

I gave him my phone, still holding on to him with one hand. He didn't look at it, not even a tiny peek, but took it, and his own and the forgotten pizza menu, and placed them all on the scarred coffee table in front of the couch. He even put both phones face down on the table.

"Won't Andy be whiny if he has to wait for dinner?" I said as Lucas, with the ease and grace of an athlete, lifted his other leg and straddled me. Each of his knees were now on the couch, and had me encaged. A cage I was dying to fly into and lock the door behind me.

"I'm willing to put up with an Andy fit if it means I can put my hands on you that much sooner," he said as he towered over me. He smiled down at me and I let out an answering sigh, my body melting all the more.

"Me too," I said quietly as I sank further down into the couch. I laid my hands on his legs. The denim of his jeans felt rough and cool, and I was vaguely surprised to not feel his body burning up the way mine seemed to be. I slid my hands up his rock-solid thighs, circling around to his ass.

He just looked down at me, but his eyes burned and his nostrils flared as if he could smell me. He probably could—I seemed to be emitting pheromones like I'd just been swimming in them instead of the IM pool.

"We can't…go very far," he said, his voice low and throaty. He cleared his throat and continued, "Seriously. Andy will wake up soon and come running out here. And I just don't want to have that talk with him quite yet about why his big brother was naked and on top of Miss Lily." An ever-so-small smile crept across his face even as he undressed me with his eyes, paying particular interest to my chest, and that strip of skin showing below my shirt.

"Okay. So no Naked Big Brother and Miss Lily," I said. I

dropped one hand from his ass and I swore I saw him flinch from the loss. I touched the hem of my shirt, brushing the back of my hand across my bare tummy.

Lucas made me want to step out of my passivity. Made me want to be bold. Made me want to stop being the peacemaker and instead be the fire starter. "So, just how far *can* we go?" My thumb slipped beneath the cool knit cotton of my white shirt, Lucas's eyes following the motion.

He swallowed hard. I followed the motion with my eyes as it traveled down his throat, wanting to lick that exact spot.

"God. So not far enough," he said. He reached over his shoulder and pulled his hoodie over his head, taking his T-shirt with it. Instinctively I reached out and hung on to the gray cotton T-shirt as he got rid of the hoodie and tossed it on the chair, on top of my jacket.

"What was I thinking?" I said as I pushed the T-shirt up his body, admiring his hard abs like I had when I'd first seen him in his board shorts at the pool. "Get rid of this too." I smoothed across his chest, the T-shirt falling over my hand, hanging up on my wrist. It didn't matter. I could now feel that gloriously warm skin. The only thing better would be to feel it against my bare chest.

"That whole Naked Big Brother thing, remember?" he said, chuckling, as he lowered and adjusted the T-shirt back into place. But he didn't move my hand. Instead he placed his on top of mine, but outside of his shirt.

"Jesus, Lily," he whispered, looking down at me, into my eyes, which surely showed how much I wanted him. "You make me so hard. You drive me crazy. From the first time I saw you."

I looked from his face to the bulge at the front of his jeans. My eyes went back to his. "Me too. From the first time I saw you."

He nodded. He knew. Of course he knew. "That first time," he said, like it had been months ago instead of just days. "When I saw you in your swimsuit, all I could think of was peeling it off you, getting inside you." He made no move, just kept my hand beneath his, his other hand gently laid on my hip. Then he sat back on his haunches, his ass resting on my legs. His fingers twined with mine, even with the cotton of his shirt between us. His other hand squeezed my hip, then his fingers splayed wide.

"Then I watched you with Andy, with all those kids. And it became more than just wanting to get in your pants." A finger smoothed along the edge of my pants, half on the material of my leggings, half on my skin. He left a trail of fire as he gently brushed that finger along my waistband. "Believe me, I still want to get in your pants. But I want to…" He sighed. I could tell these types of words were hard for a guy like Lucas. Which made me treasure them all the more. I waited for him to continue, lying quietly beneath him, my hands still on his body. "I want to *know* you, Lily Spaulding. Really know you." I squeezed the hand that held mine. He took a deep breath then let it out. "And…I want you to know me, too."

I waited, wanting him to know that I got how hard that was for him to say. "I want that too," I said, meaning it more than anything I'd ever said before.

NINE

❖

IT WAS a good thing that Lucas insisted on the no Naked Big Brother thing, because Andy came bounding out of his room soon after Lucas proclaimed he wanted to get to know me.

A proclamation that shouldn't seem like that big of a deal, granted. But it was. With Lucas it absolutely was.

I instinctively knew he didn't say that to just anybody. Yeah, he could have been totally playing me. But, gorgeous as he was, Lucas didn't seem to be a player. If anything, I could see that title falling more to Stick than Lucas.

When Lucas heard Andy's door opening—way before I did—he was off me with the speed that had earned him a scholarship to USC. Before Andy's little legs had carried him down the hallway, Lucas was on the other side of the couch from me with the pizza menu and phone in his hands.

We ordered the pizza and we all wolfed it down, demolishing two larges. Now that I knew I wouldn't be getting naked with Lucas tonight, I let my appetite run wild, and yeah, probably sublimated one appetite to another.

From the look on Lucas's face as he watched me lick the grease from my lips, then sank his teeth into the thick crust, he was too.

We watched a kid-friendly movie, Andy tucked between us on the couch. I couldn't even tell you what we watched; my concentration was so not on the television. Lucas had pulled my bun loose as we'd made our way from the kitchen to the couch, and throughout the entire movie he had his arm across the back of the couch, behind Andy, and his hand played with my hair.

His look of regret over Andy's head told me this wasn't how he'd pictured the first time he'd get my hair long and loose and lying with him on his couch.

Having a six-year-old kick me in the hip every time one of the cartoon minions did something funny wasn't exactly how I'd fantasized about it, either.

Around nine, Andy started conking out and Lucas woke him up enough to get him to brush his teeth, put on his jammies, and say goodnight to Miss Lily. At the last, Andy seemed to come alive, and ran down the short hallway and launched himself into my arms, his skinny arms wrapping around my neck, much like they did when he didn't want to go under water.

But there was no trepidation now, just pure little-kid emotion. And it was all pointed at me. "Thanks, Lily," he said, smacking me on the cheek. "Thanks for going swimming with us." He didn't let go, and I hugged him tighter to me.

I had to admit it felt good. Until the night Lucas had kissed me in front of the graffiti, I hadn't been touched—at least deeply touched—since my parents had dropped me off at Bribury and my mom had held on tightly as she'd hugged me goodbye.

That day I'd been eager for them to get on the road, not wanting to hear any more of my father's instructions on how to "handle" Jane. But about a week later, when the only other human contact I felt had been quick handshakes with new people, I'd wished I hadn't shed my mom's hug quite so quickly.

I rubbed Andy's little back, the worn cotton of his pajamas soft and smelling like fabric softener.

"Okay, buddy, say goodnight and let's get to bed," Lucas said, his voice soft but firm.

Andy untangled from me—or me from him—and gave me another peck on the cheek. "See you next lesson," he said, and returned down the hall.

"Yep, see you Tuesday," I called after him, not really sure if kids his age had a good concept of how many days away Tuesday was.

Lucas disappeared with Andy into his room, then came out about twenty minutes later.

"Sorry," he said as he moved to the kitchen and started cleaning up the empty pizza boxes. "We had to do an encore of *Where the Wild Things Are* tonight. Apparently once just wasn't enough." He moved the dirty plates to the sink, running water over them, but leaving them. He wiped off the table with a dishrag.

It was mesmerizing to watch this god of a man do mundane household tasks. He would seem so much more at home…on a football field, I suppose.

And yet…this Lucas was maybe even more attractive. How he was with Andy? Total turn-on, I have to admit, even though I was in no way looking for a guy with as much responsibility as it seemed Lucas was dealing with.

Although the male population of Bribury, rich and entitled as they were—as we *all* were—certainly hadn't made my pulse jump off the charts like seeing Lucas in swim trunks had.

"That's okay," I said. "I'm just surprised he'd be able to stay awake for two readings, after all the swimming and pizza."

Lucas looked a little embarrassed. "I think he fell asleep right after I started the second reading, I just didn't realize it until I was done. I need to start looking at him more frequently when I'm reading to him." He said the last almost to himself, as if trying to make a mental note.

He came and sat on the couch beside me, in the space Andy had occupied. But he didn't make a move toward me, he just seem content to sit together. I wrapped my hand in his, content as well.

"This is all new to you, then? Putting Andy to bed? Being the one to take him to swim lessons?"

He stretched out his long legs, put one hand behind his head for a pillow. "Yeah, I promised you the Life and Times of Lucas Kade, didn't I?"

"You did, but I can take a rain check if you want."

He shook his head, just a tiny bit, his silky black hair brushing his jaw. "Nah, might as well be tonight. As long as we aren't going to get naked…" He looked at me with a grin, waggling his eyebrows.

"You're the one who said we'd scare the children," I said, teasing.

He let out an exaggerated sigh. "Yes, we mustn't harm the children. They're so impressionable at this age."

I waited, a smile of encouragement on my face.

He sighed again, but this wasn't exaggerated, it was resigned. "Okay. Let's see. Why I'm here taking care of Andy first, or why I'm back in Schoolport and not in the running for the Heisman?" There was bitterness in his voice. I'd heard it before, and it seemed out of place on him. He seemed to have more…peace about his current situation (whatever it was) than most guys I knew would.

"Let's start with Andy and work backwards," I said, trying to steer him toward what I thought would be safer ground. The small smile that crossed his face as I mentioned Andy's name confirmed my choice.

"He's a great kid, right?" he asked. And it really was asking; he didn't seem at all sure.

"Yeah, he's great."

He turned toward me, and draped his arm across the back of the couch behind my head. He placed his other hand on my knee. "You're around other kids his age, other kids that are in kind of the same…situation. Is Andy doing okay? Is he, I don't know, keeping up?"

"You mean with swimming? I mean, he's not too keen to go under water, but that's usually about half the class of kids his age who haven't swum before."

He was nodding with my words. "Right. Right. And we're working on that. Did you see him today? He went under quite a bit."

I smiled, remembering Andy's proclamation. "Four times."

Lucas chuckled. "Right. Four times." He looked toward the kitchen, then down at his work boots. "But what about non-swimming? Does he seem, like, more messed up than any of the other kids?"

Oh man, we were getting into territory I had no business going into. "I don't…I'm not really—"

"I mean, his teacher says he's doing well, that he's keeping up with the other kids academically." His voice turned to a little sarcasm as he added, "Though I don't know how the hell they measure academics in first grade." His face sobered. "But they do, right? I guess I should know how that's measured, right?"

I put a hand on top of his, still resting on my knee. I could feel his tension, see it in the set of his wide shoulders.

"His teacher will tell you that," I said. "If they say he's doing well, he is. They'd definitely let you know if there was something…" I didn't want to say the word "wrong," and yet that was what this all seemed to be pointing to—something had gone wrong in Andy's life, and Lucas was hoping it hadn't permanently affected the kid.

"So, this is all new for you? Watching Andy, taking care of him?"

He nodded, his eyes still downcast, his head bowed. I longed to reach out and stroke his head, pull him to my chest, but I stayed still.

"Yeah, it's all new. Well, at least the living here." He swept his arm, encompassing the small room. "I've tried to be in Andy's life since he was born. But the past few years I've been kind of… checked out."

"Because you were in California? At USC?"

He nodded, not looking at me. "That. Yeah, at first, that." His shoulders tensed, hunched slightly. "But then…" He looked over at me. "Just how much do you know from wherever you heard it?"

There was no censure in his voice, just a simple question. "I googled you and it said you were highly sought after and went to

USC, but left in your junior year after a bad injury. Shoulder, I think?"

He nodded. I thought back to seeing him in the pool. I hadn't noticed any huge scar anywhere. "You had surgery?" He nodded again. "But that didn't help?"

He sat back, sinking deeper into the couch. He moved his hands to cover his face, then lowered them, as if he knew he couldn't hide from whatever he was about to say.

"It helped. Who knows? Maybe I would have played again, but I fucked up."

I held my tongue, though of course I was dying to ask.

"I got into…um…" He took a deep breath and turned his body to face me. Really face me. "I got hooked on Oxy after my surgery. I got kicked out of school."

Wow. I was thinking maybe he got caught cheating on a test to keep up academically or something. A drug habit was beyond my scope. This was a little more than I'd bargained for.

I looked into his eyes, waiting for these strong feelings—which had blossomed so quickly and become so intense—to fade or wilt with the news that he had been (is?) a drug addict.

They didn't. If anything, they deepened, knowing that Lucas was more than just a gorgeous guy who was stepping up with his little brother. He had lived, and *changed*, much like I had suspected Syd had.

"Go on," I said.

His shoulders lowered a bit and he licked his lips. I squeezed his hand. "Go on, Lucas. I'm still here. I'm *staying* here."

"Jesus, Lily," he said in a mere whisper. "I think I just fell a little bit in love with you." His eyes didn't leave mine, and I tried to convey what I could not say.

I was already more than a little bit in love with Lucas Kade.

"Anyway. Word got out. I suppose it wouldn't have looked good for a player—former player—to become hooked on painkillers. They agreed to keep it quiet if I just left school quietly and relinquished my scholarship. I was done with football, anyway. The shoulder wouldn't hold up."

"Could you have at least stayed to get your degree? Could you have—"

He held up a hand to stop me. "No. By that time I wanted to come home. I knew I could…"

"Get drugs here," I finished when he didn't.

He nodded, breaking eye contact, but still stayed turned toward me, still let me hold his hand.

"Oh yeah, the Oxy was easy to get here. I could have called a dozen guys and they'd be on my doorstep in an hour, happy to hand me those awesome pills."

"But you had to pay for them," I said, leading him to the inevitable.

"Yep. And I did…for a while. It was just a matter of time before I got caught or died, or needed something stronger and jumped to heroin or something."

I'd been around drugs in high school. But that was more like pot and the occasional line of cocaine that was rumored to be snorted in the bathroom at a party. Sometimes you'd hear about a kid raiding their parents' medicine cabinet and having a mystery pill-swap party. Ecstasy in clubs, stuff like that. Party drugs. Nothing that was going to derail the oh-so-promising progeny of the political world.

Certainly not heroin.

"But then something happened. My mom…she'd always had…*problems* with drugs."

"I only saw her a few times at Andy's lessons. And I never even spoke with her."

"Yeah, she got him there, which was about the last thing she was able to handle. She went into rehab a couple of days later and I moved in here."

"So, you've only been…clean five weeks?" I had no idea if "clean" was the word I was looking for. I knew the first time I saw him that I was out of my depth with Lucas Kade, but I now knew I was in way over my head.

No lifeguarding experience was going to save me this time.

"No. Six months. I haven't used in six months. About the same time I realized my mom had started using again. And about the same time I…"

"Yes?"

He shook his head, and I knew I wasn't going to hear about all the things Lucas did to get money for his habit. Or to buy huge flat-screens.

"It doesn't matter. I knew I had to get my shit together. I didn't do it for me, but I could do it for Andy. That poor kid had it worse than I did at that age, and I just wanted to, I don't know, give him a chance, I guess."

"So you quit the Oxy? Just like that?"

He chuckled. The sound seemed foreign and jarring in the quiet room with such a heavy topic. "Well, not 'just like that,' no. It was pretty shitty for a while. But I made it out the other side. Eventually."

"And…the other stuff? The stuff to get the money?"

"Well, that wasn't as easy to quit because it didn't affect just me. I had *interested* parties in me still needing money, and they weren't happy."

"Stick."

He shrugged. "Stick's okay. He stood behind me, still does. It was more of the people Stick works for."

Visions of every mafia movie I'd ever watched with my father played in my mind. "Just how…deep are you in?"

"I'm not. I'm out. I was never 'in' much, anyway, just a… runner, an information gatherer, a cog. There was another guy who needed money right behind me. Shit, there were thirty guys behind me. There are *always* young guys who need money that are willing to do anything to get it."

"Anything?"

He waved a hand. "No, it wasn't anything heavy. I don't mean to scare you, Lily. It was kid stuff in the scheme of things."

"So…" I needed him to say it, even if I couldn't ask it.

"Nothing that hurt anyone. Cars, money, some property. Everything was insured. And it was from people who could afford it."

"My family are people like that," I said. "My family works very hard for their car, property and money."

"I know," he said softly. "I didn't mean it like that. It was wrong. Of course I know it was wrong. I just didn't want you to think I was out whacking people or anything."

I nodded. I knew the difference. And I also knew that Lucas didn't need to tell me any of this, didn't have to be so honest. He was either telling this all to me to scare me away, or…or…because he was in as deep as I was and didn't want anything between us.

"And you're completely done with it? With all of it?"

"Yes." I could hear the conviction in his voice. It was the truth, or at least he desperately wanted it to be.

So did I.

"Over. Done. When I saw my mom was back using, I started hanging around here more, making sure she got to work, and that Andy was taken care of. They found out about it where she worked and she was given the choice of going to rehab or being fired. Which probably saved her life. I had some money from… before, and was able to help out for a while.

"Then I got on at Bribury. I was able to do third shift 'cause it pays more. It sucks, but it's honest work and the benefits are good." He smiled. "Shit, listen to me talking about benefits. I sound like an old man."

"No," I said, running my hand up and down his arm. "You sound like someone who has responsibilities."

He took my hand, raised it to his mouth, and turned it to kiss my palm.

"How's your mom doing?"

A shadow crossed his face. "I'm not really sure. They're still in the no-contact phase." He said this like I knew the phases of rehab. "I'll get to see her in a week. She wasn't happy about going, but it was the only way to keep her job. And I was moving in to take care of Andy.

"That was another reason I wanted third shift; it was great hours for Andy's schedule. I can take him to school, sleep while he's there, then pick him up. Some days he does the swim lessons, others we just come home. I get him dinner and to bed. When I have to go to work, my neighbor, Mrs. Jankowski, comes and sleeps here."

"Wow, that's nice of her."

He shrugged. "We have a deal. I do some repairs for her and do her grocery shopping and errands and shit like that. She's not big on leaving the building."

"That's really great of you to move back in here to help out."

"The truth is, it's probably saving my life. I knew this was coming as soon as I saw my mom was in trouble. She's been fighting it, on and off, most of my life.

"I was either going to go down the same path, or turn it around right then. Andy made me take a good look at where I was headed."

"And your father? And Andy's?"

"My dad died when I was twelve. Gunshot. Andy's dad is out of the picture. Has been since the married asshole ran out on my mom once he knocked her up."

"Oh," I said. "That sucks."

He put both his hands on my face, cradling it. "I want you to know, Lily, that I would never do something like that. We'll be careful and shit, but if you ever…if *we* ever…I would never leave you high and dry."

"I know you wouldn't," I said, looking into his pleading eyes. "I know you wouldn't, Lucas."

Although the last thing I wanted to think about as a freshman in college was an unwanted pregnancy, I knew that if I was pregnant with his child that Lucas would step up like he had for Andy.

"And thank you for telling me all this. You didn't have to."

He rested his forehead on mine, still holding on to my face

with strong, callused hands. "Yes, I did, Lily. Yes, I did."

He kissed me, so, so sweetly. It was a kiss full of thanks and acceptance, and I returned it with all the emotions that swirled inside me. I placed my hands on his soft T-shirt, on his chest and abs, feeling his body tense and jump under my touch.

"Lily," he whispered, breaking the kiss, then resuming it with a deeper, probing, devouring melding of mouths and lips. "God, Lily."

I slid my hands under his tee, needing to feel his skin. "How deeply does Andy sleep?" I murmured when Lucas left my mouth and began kissing down my neck.

"Not deeply enough. Not for all the things I want to do to you. Not for how much I want to make you scream my name." As if to prove his point, he nipped at my neck and I let out a moan. A none-too-soft moan at that.

"See?" he said, chuckling, then returned to my neck, his hands sliding from my face down my body, stopping at my waist, where he tugged me toward him.

I swung a leg over and straddled him, finally in the position I'd wanted to be in that night in the back seat of Stick's car. He sank into the back of the couch, only leaning forward when I tugged at his shirt. He lifted his arms and I peeled the offending cotton off of him, again marveling at the sheer perfection of him. And now, I could see the tiny scar at his shoulder. I leaned forward and placed a kiss on it, then continued to strew kisses along his amazing chest, swirling my tongue around his nipples.

He smelled faintly of chlorine and the soap they have in dispensers in the showers at the IM building.

"Christ, Lily, you're killing me. We really can't."

"I know. We'll stop," I said, not wanting to.

"Not yet…not yet," he whispered, his hands now leaving my waist and anchoring in my hair. "God, I knew it would be fucking amazing," he said, wrapping his hands deep in it, tugging gently.

I raised my head from his chest, sat up tall. He dropped his hands still holding my hair, causing me to tilt my chin up.

"Christ, you're beautiful," he whispered.

I looked down at him. "So are you," I said, then ducked my head, needing to kiss him again.

And cursing that cute little boy sleeping in the next room.

It wasn't the little boy that drew our session to a swift conclusion, but the noise of a key in the lock and the front door opening.

Before I had even registered what was happening, Lucas had me off his lap and was placing his body in front of mine, even though I had all my clothes on and he was the one naked from the waist up.

It had me wondering who—or what—would walk in Lucas's front door that he felt he needed to protect me from.

TEN

※

"KNOCK MUCH, asshole?" Lucas said to Stick as he entered the apartment.

"I thought I'd wake up Andy," Stick said in a soft voice matching Lucas's. "Hey, Lily," he said in my direction.

"Hi, Stick," I replied as Lucas moved away from me, grabbing his T-shirt from the couch and, sadly, putting it back on.

"You couldn't text that you were about to go all B&E on me?"

"It's not exactly B&E if I have the keys," Stick said, jingling his keychain before shoving it in his jeans pocket. "Besides, I needed to talk to you."

I didn't mention that talking to Lucas could be accomplished via phone. And then my suspicious mind took the turn that perhaps what Stick wanted to talk to Lucas about should not be done on a phone or with texts.

Was Lucas telling me the truth? Was he done with that life?

"There's nothing that we have to talk about that can't be said on a phone," Lucas said, as if reading my thoughts. Or maybe my skeptical look.

"Let's go into your room for a sec," Stick said, starting down the hallway, not even stopping in the living room.

"No," Lucas said, still sitting on the couch with me. Stick turned around and gave Lucas a pointed look. "I mean it, Stick. No. I just got done telling Lily that I wasn't doing...anything I shouldn't anymore."

Stick looked at me with a look I couldn't quite decipher. Partially pissed off, yes. But also with an almost grudging respect. "Do you think that was a good idea?" he asked Lucas. He made his way back to the living room, sitting in a beat-up chair to the side of the couch.

"I trust Lily," Lucas said.

"Yes, but now I have to, too."

"You can," Lucas and I said at the same time.

I rose from the couch, hating to leave Lucas's warm body beside me, but knowing that the whole vibe of the evening had completely changed—first with Lucas's story, and now with Stick showing up. "I think I'm going to take off. It's getting late."

"So many frat boys with roofies to do, so little time," Stick said, moving his legs so I could pass by him.

"Shut up, Stick," Lucas and I both said at the same time. Lucas rose and came after me. "Lily, you don't have to leave." He gently held my arm, and I would have loved nothing more than to sink back into his hold, into him. But instead I smiled and said, "I know I don't have to, but it's late, and umm, maybe it's better to not have so much…temptation with Andy in the next room and all."

"Right. Right." Lucas nodded, glancing down the hallway to where Andy slept. "No Naked Big Brother. Got it."

Stick wisely kept his mouth shut at this, and I just nodded and stepped into Lucas's arms, which quickly encircled me. I wrapped my arms around his neck and went on my tiptoes to kiss him lightly. "Call me tomorrow," I said. "If you want," I added.

"Oh, I want," he said. "I want very bad."

I smiled. "Me too," I whispered against his mouth, kissing him one last time.

Stepping away from him, I crossed to my backpack and pulled out my phone. "Do you have a number for a cab? Or is there a bus stand nearby?" I knew he couldn't leave Andy there alone.

"You do not want to stand in this neighborhood for a bus this time of night," Stick said, rising from the chair. "I'll give you a ride to your dorm. Or wherever you're going."

"To my dorm. And I can take a cab. I'll just find a number for one." I started scrolling my phone when Lucas put a hand on mine, stilling my motions.

"No cab is going to come here, either. I can have Stick stay here with Andy and I can give you a ride."

For some reason, I didn't want Stick to be here when Lucas got home from dropping me off. Didn't want Stick to have unlimited time to try and convince Lucas to do whatever plan Stick had come here with.

"That's okay," I said, and turned to Stick. "Your offer still stand?"

"Yeah, can you just give me a second alone with Lucas first?"

Lucas was about to object, but I laid a hand on his chest, the same chest that only moments ago was naked and I was caressing with my mouth. "Sure. I need to use the restroom anyway."

I made my way down the hallway, feeling both sets of eyes on me. Lucas probably watching my ass. Stick probably waiting for me to close the door.

Not even waiting. "Dude, this is a no-brainer. Zero risk. And—" That was all I heard before I shut the bathroom door. I wished it wouldn't have been so obvious with them both watching, or I would have left it open a crack.

And for a small apartment in a shitty part of town, the bathroom door was surprisingly, frustratingly, thick and soundproof.

Taking care of business as quickly as I could, I reentered the living room to see a pissed-off Stick and an at-ease Lucas, and the sight gave me a small rush of relief.

I cared what Lucas did before we met, of course. But what really mattered to me was the man he was now, and that man was taking a shitty job so he'd be able to keep his kid brother in a stable situation.

That was enough for me. For now.

Lucas gave me a goodnight kiss that had me silent for the first five minutes of the ride home with Stick.

Finally, as we made our way through town to campus, he said, "Are we really going to your dorm, or do you want to be dropped somewhere else?"

"My dorm. Like I said."

He shrugged. "I don't give a shit. And I won't tell Lucas if you wanted to be dropped at whatever big bash the Bribury elite are gathering at tonight."

I looked at him for a second as he stared at the road. "Are you asking me if Jane is at a party?"

His snort of disgust assured me I'd made a direct hit. "Yeah. Right. Like I give a shit what little Miss Silver Spoon is doing tonight."

"You have her wrong, you know. She said the other night half a silver spoon, but what she didn't say is that spoon was kept away from her, used like a bargaining chip her whole life."

"Poor baby." His voice was dripping with condescension.

"Some said so, yes."

He looked over at me then. "What do you mean? Who the hell is Jane Winters anyway?"

I shrugged. "Not my story to tell." I pulled my phone out and dialed, putting it on speaker.

"Where the hell are you?" Jane's voice, slightly slurred, came through. Loud music played in the background. It sounded like some kind of EDM, not the usual folk-lite stuff that played at the smaller parties we'd gone to. "We're having an *amazing* time, get your ass over here."

"Where are you exactly?" I asked, now wishing I hadn't put the speaker on. But it was a small car and Jane was speaking so loudly that Stick would have heard anyway.

"At that club in Chesney that Heather told us about."

"How'd you get in?" I asked. Fake IDs weren't unheard of, but if Jane had one and got busted, and I didn't even know about it…I didn't even want to imagine the shit storm that my father would rain down on me.

"Jane? How'd you get in?" I asked again.

"Pffft. Easy peasy. You have got to come, Lily, the dancing is hype."

"Shit," I said to myself. Stick gave me a questioning look. "Is Syd with you?"

"No. But Lily, you'll never guess who's here. Montrose! Can you believe it? I am so going to hit that tonight. He's going to be late for class for sure on Monday—'cause he won't be able to walk!" She laughed loud and boisterously at that. I loved Jane when she was "on" like this. She was free and daring and brave, all things I wished I could be. But being drunk and underage at a club was not a smart move. And with Montrose there too…

"Would you mind if—" I said to Stick, but he was already turning off the route to the dorm and away from town, toward Chesney, a wealthy town about twenty minutes from Schoolport. Most of the faculty from Bribury lived in Chesney, not deigning to live in the crappy town where they worked.

"I'm not sure I can get in," I said when we'd reached Chesney and the club where Jane was partying.

"Don't worry about it. Keep the motor running," he said as he left the car double-parked in front of the club. "Christ, this is really fucking up my night," I heard him say to himself as he shut the car door behind him.

The bouncer approached Stick, motioning to the car. Stick wasn't as big and broad as Lucas, but he wasn't tiny, either. But he was dwarfed by the huge bouncer, who towered over him. He placed a meaty finger in Stick's chest and again motioned to the car where I sat.

I couldn't hear them, even if I had rolled down the window—and I didn't particularly want to. But I could see Stick chatting up the bouncer, waving a hand to me, then a hand at the club.

The bouncer looked pissed (do bouncers look any other way on a Saturday night?), but eventually stepped back and waved

Stick into the club.

I sat, debating whether to call Jane again and let her know Stick was coming to get her. Not even knowing whom she was with, I figured a surprise attack from Stick might be the best approach.

It seemed to take forever, and the bouncer glared at me the whole time, while occasionally letting in new arrivals. I noticed everyone who went in was well into their late twenties or thirties, and dressed in expensive club clothes.

This was not a college club, even for those students over twenty-one.

Good God, if my father found out about this. Stick came out then with Jane in tow. Literally towing her, her arm firmly in his grasp.

She said something to the bouncer, and he stepped forward for a second, as if to answer Jane's appeal, until Stick said something. The bouncer left Jane to Stick and sat back down on his stool.

"Lily," she yelled in my ear, wrapping her arms around me as I stepped out of the car to let Jane get in the back seat. "You need to come inside with me. The DJ is totally sick, and I'm soooo close to hooking up with Montrose." She looked across the hood at Stick, who was crossing over to the driver's side.

"Until this asshole showed up." She yanked on my arm. "C'mon, Lily. Come back inside with me."

"We need to get home, Jane," I said, trying to guide her unwilling body to the back seat.

She stumbled a bit and her whole body seemed to heave.

"Unh huh," Stick said, now sitting behind the wheel. "She is not going to chuck in my car."

"I don't 'chuck,'" Jane said.

"Yeah, sure you don't. No college freshman getting hammered for the first time ever does," he said, almost to himself.

"It's not the first—"

"You'll have to put her in the front seat, Lily," Stick said to me, as if Jane was a bag of groceries. "Less chance of her getting sick than riding in the back."

I was all for leaving the deadweight of Jane with Stick. I sat her in the front seat and Stick held on to her arm as I eased the seat forward as much as possible with her in it. I squeezed into the back, then put the front seat back into position, Jane flopping back with it.

I tried to reach through the opening, but couldn't reach the door to shut it.

Noticing my inability to get us on our way, Stick softly swore, then moved across the bench front seat, reaching past Jane, and pulled the door close.

That perked the fading Jane back up. "Boob graze! Totally felt that boob graze, ya perv."

"Yeah, highlight of my night," Stick said with disgust. "Grazing your tits has totally made this shitty night worthwhile."

"Well, they are very nice tits," Jane said, letting her head fall back on the headrest and closing her eyes.

A tiny chuckle escaped Stick, almost unwillingly. "Keep your eyes open," he said to Jane in an almost nice voice. "Less chance of getting sick. And buckle up so you don't fall and crack your skull on my dash."

Jane struggled with the seatbelt, needing several tries to make it click. Stick sighed with disgust.

I slid over behind Stick so I could keep a better watch on Jane. Remarkably, she listened to Stick and opened her eyes. Even managed to hold her head straight.

"Jane, how did you even get in there?" I asked. "Who were you with?"

She waved a hand in the air, like coming to be in a much-older club at eighteen was nothing. Maybe it was to Jane. I didn't know a lot about her life before Bribury, though I was sure my father would have briefed me on anything...dangerous, if he'd been aware.

"Oh, my lovely Lily," Jane said, not so much slurring her words as singing them. "You don't get to know everything. Don't want you reporting it back to Daddy, do we?"

I stiffened. "I thought we were good the night we did the True Confessions thing," I said. "You know I wouldn't—"

"Why the fuck would Lily tell *her* father you got drunk?" Stick interrupted as he drove us away from Chesney and back to Schoolport.

"I wouldn't. I don't…" But I let the words trail off. I didn't want to lie to Jane, and I honestly wasn't sure what I would say to my father about this night.

"Because Lily—poor, poor, beautiful Lily—has been sent to Bribury to be my keeper. An unofficial Secret Service agent, if you will."

"I…I'm not…" Again, I couldn't finish.

"'S'okay," she said. "We're good. All is cool. No worries."

She looked over her shoulder at me, her eyes glassy, but I could still see the brilliant intelligence behind them. "You're just a pawn in this game, Lily, and I get that." She reached her hand across the back seat and I instinctively reached for it. She squeezed my hand, then released me, facing forward again. "You probably didn't even want to go to Bribury, did you, Lily?"

I sat back in my seat, soaking in Jane's words. "No," I said softly. I had wanted to go to Maryland.

"Poor, beautiful Lily," Jane said again.

I felt the beginnings of something stir in me. I had tamped down all my anger about not being able to go to the college of my choice, about having to go to Bribury, room with Jane. I told myself that I was just being a good daughter, that I was lucky to even have this opportunity that so many kids didn't.

But I was pissed off. And I didn't get pissed off. I was the good daughter, the peacemaker, the girl people pointed to and said, "What a great girl you have there, Grayson," and I would bask in it.

But I wasn't that girl anymore. I could feel a change in myself. Had it started with Lucas, or was totally inappropriate Lucas a by-product of it?

We drove in silence for a while, each digesting our own thoughts after Jane's semi-confession. Finally, as we neared campus, Stick asked the same question he asked of me earlier. "Just who the fuck are you, Jane Winters?"

Jane had once again rested her head on the headrest, and she turned her head toward Stick, studying him. He met her eyes and it seemed like both of their guards dropped for just a second. Then Jane turned her head forward again, and closed her eyes.

"Nobody," she said. Then she whispered, "God, I'm dying to be fucking nobody."

ELEVEN

·⊰⊱·

WE SPENT Sunday in our room, me only going out to the convenience store that sat on the edge of campus to buy supplies for the day—ice pack for Jane's head, saltines and ginger ale, stuff like that. We ordered a pizza later in the day after Jane felt like eating.

"You don't have to babysit me, Lily," she said throughout the day. "I can't get up to any illegal hijinks in this shape. You can have the day off."

"I'm good," I said. And I was. I didn't want to go anywhere in case…yes, in case Lucas called. Not that I wouldn't get his call no matter where I was, but I wanted to be where he knew I lived in case he wanted to get together on short notice. So, other than the quick run to the 7-Eleven, I was staying in the room with Jane all day.

Yes, I knew it was pathetic, but I wasn't quite so desperate to see him that I called him. I at least left that up to him. Last night he'd said he very much wanted to call me today. But as the day dwindled, I got edgier and edgier. I made a pretense of wanting to be in the room to study.

Syd came over for most of the day. Once seeing Jane's condition, she left for an hour, then come back bearing some crazy concoction that she swore was good for hangovers. Jane looked at it skeptically, but drank it, and it seemed to do the trick. We lay on our beds, Syd camped out on mine, and did postmortems of the previous night.

With both Jane and me AWOL, Syd had gone to another party that our friend Jeff had told her about. I suppose hoping that Jeff's older brother would be there, though she didn't add that part.

"Hook up with anybody?" Jane asked her.

Syd shook her head, her gorgeous black hair rippling. Every girl practically, except Jane, had long hair. Most of us wore ours up on days like this, in ponytails or buns, just casual. But Syd always wore her straight black hair down, loose and straightened, even on a lazy, casual day like this. In so many ways she tried to copy all the other girls, but not in this.

"I *talked* with this guy for a while, but…"

"How much did you *talk*?" Jane asked, not afraid to push, when I probably would have left it at that.

"Talking" and "hooking up" were done in varying degrees, and it could be anything from actual talking to full-blown sex on the hood of a car in the middle of a crowded parking lot.

"Just some kissing," Syd said. "Maybe a little more."

Jane's eyes lit up, and she propped her head up with her hand, elbow bent, lying on her side. "You ho bag. Tell us everything."

Syd flopped down beside me on the bed. "Nothing to tell. Like I said, a little more than kissing."

"Details," Jane yelled, tossing a throw pillow at Syd. Syd ducked, of course, and the pillow hit me instead.

"Oh, you know," Syd said casually. "Nothing the two of you weren't probably doing. A little fumbling below clothes is all. I started to give him a hand job, but he wanted a blowie and I just wasn't into him enough to make the effort."

Jane nodded as if agreeing, then rolled onto her back, staring up at the ceiling. "Damn, I was so close to bagging Montrose. I would have totally given *him* a blowie."

I felt Syd stiffen next to me. She knew Jane's story, and must have realized what a colossal fuck-up Jane blowing her prof would be. Especially if people were around and saw them leave together.

The kids our age at Bribury were too young to know who Jane was, or know her story. But those people at that club last night were probably old enough to put it together. Hell, it's a wonder Montrose didn't know who she was.

Maybe he did.

"Jane, just how much time did you spend with Montrose last night?"

"Clearly not enough," Jane said, pouting.

"Yeah, but before we got there? Were you, like, *with* him? With the group he was with?"

"Who was he there with?" Syd asked, asking a question I didn't care about. I wanted to know what Jane had done.

"Relax. No pictures are on anybody's phones."

"Yeah, but—"

"I didn't get that close to him, okay?" she said, a bit embarrassed. "I tried to get him to dance with me, but he turned me down. Totally ignored me."

Syd's body relaxed, as did my fear. And I knew I wouldn't need to tell my father about Jane's night of clubbing.

But I knew I wouldn't have anyway. I knew I was stepping away from my father's every command, becoming my own person.

I suppose that's what college is about…becoming your own self, shedding who you were.

Again I wondered if that was what Lucas was to me—a way to rebel, a way to test myself, a way to move away from the hold my parents had on me.

And yet Lucas didn't feel like a rebellion. He felt like comfort and safety, even though I knew the life he led, and the world he lived in, were anything but safe and comfortable.

I just knew what I felt for him was beyond the way he made my body tremble when he put his hands on me, or the way his eyes burned into mine just before he kissed me.

After hearing his story last night, all he'd gone through, how he'd turned his life around after the Oxy, and was now taking care of Andy while his mother got clean…I had thought it before, but now I knew I was in deep with Lucas.

I had looked forward to doing the casual hookup thing that was so prevalent here at Bribury. Nobody actually *dated*. You "talked," you "hooked up," you "hung out," and it was all good. You were able to meet lots of people that way, with no expectations, and no hurt feelings.

Certainly with no wasted Sundays waiting for someone to call.

And I had wanted that, had embraced the casual culture after coming from a high school that was all about traditional "going out" coupling.

But now…now I just wanted the damn phone to ring.

"Why don't you just call him?" Jane said, as if she could read my mind.

"It's not that big of a deal," I lied. "He's got to work later tonight, anyway. We kept it casual."

Jane snorted at that. Syd reached a hand behind herself and patted my hip.

We sat in comfortable silence for a while, until Jane said again, almost to herself, "I was so close to gettin' with Montrose."

"Give it a rest," Syd said in a lazy voice. She was nearing sleep, and I wished I could doze into a nap like that. But no, I lay quietly next to Syd, praying for my phone to buzz.

But it never did.

TWELVE

※

SYD HAD a class earlier than our Montrose class on Monday mornings, so Jane and I always just met her there, taking our time in the morning and having a bigger breakfast at the caf.

Or at least we usually did. Jane's stomach was still shaky after puking up the pizza—and Saturday night's alcohol—late last night. And my appetite had seemed to vanish.

I couldn't stand the thought of being one of those girls who couldn't function because some guy didn't call when he said he would. But I had a gut-level fear that that was exactly what I'd become.

Jane's phone buzzed and she swore as she glanced at the caller ID. We kept walking across campus, but she took the call.

"Yes?" she said, not exactly snapping, but certainly not a "hey, s'up" either.

"Mmm-hmm," she answered to whatever was being said. I had a suspicion that it was either her mother or father, simply by the way her shoulders tensed and her gait sped up, like she was trying to walk away from the caller.

I swim a few times a week and walk everywhere on this campus, and yet I became winded trying to keep up with Jane. And then I thought that maybe she was trying to ditch me, that she wanted to take this call in private. I slowed down, letting her get ahead of me.

But apparently that wasn't what she'd been trying to do,

because she stopped a few yards in front of me, waiting for me to catch up.

"It's never gonna happen," she was saying when I reached her. "I know what she said, but I'm saying no. I can do that, you know. I am over eighteen now." She listened for a moment, not moving, still standing even though I'd caught up to her. People streamed around us on the walking path. Some were kids I knew, and they gave me a nod while looking at Jane, who was becoming more and more agitated.

"Yes, you *can* do that. And you know what? Go ahead. I'm calling your bluff. I don't give a shit if I have to wash dishes to pay my way through community college. In fact, I'd almost *rather* do that than—"

Yep, definitely one of her parents. My guess was her mother. When her father called, Jane didn't get as…bitchy with him.

"Go right ahead. I'm sure the dress will look amazing on another one of Betsy's bridesmaids. Lord knows they're probably fighting over that spot at the altar."

So, not her mother. No way would Jane's mother have anything to do with Jane's half-sister Betsy's wedding plans.

Not that she wouldn't want to.

Jane was the love child (her mother's words—Jane said bastard) of Pandora Winters and Joseph Stratton. No shame in being born out of wedlock, of course. But the kicker was Joseph Stratton was married with two kids and running for president at the time he had an affair with the flighty, New Agey Pandora (not her real name, by the way, Jane told me).

It became public even though Pandora, for a while, claimed Jane wasn't Joseph's baby. Stratton and his wife tried to bluff through it, tried to weather the storm. My father, at the time Stratton's top political consultant and campaign manager, did damage control. One guy on the campaign even said Pandora's baby was his.

But it all came out, as these things always do.

Stratton withdrew from the presidential campaign and

entered the private sector. He acknowledged Jane when she was about one, much to Pandora's delight and leading to the demise of his marriage (also to Pandora's delight). Though Joseph never started back up with Pandora (to her dismay).

I knew none of this at the time, being only nine months old myself.

My father went on, being kingmaker to other politicians, but apparently always staying in touch with Joseph Stratton.

I found this all out when my father sat me down and said I was going to Bribury, would be Jane Winters' roommate, and that I needed to keep her on the straight and narrow.

I'd spent that whole night googling everything I could about Jane Winters (not much), Pandora Winters (a ton!), and Joseph Stratton (a ton and a half!).

And then I'd done what I'd always done, and said yes to my father. Not that it was really a choice, but it still felt like I was keeping a little control that way.

"Yeah, well, I am totally serious on this, Joe," Jane said now, confirming it was indeed her father on the phone. "It is nonnegotiable. And if you push on this, I'm going to skip the wedding altogether." She listened, and after a moment gave a terse "goodbye" and clicked off.

"Un-fucking-believable," she said as she looked around her, as if surprised to find herself in the middle of campus. "He is such a piece of shit." She started walking toward the building we were headed to, checking the time on her phone. "Shit, now we're going to be late," she said, picking up the pace.

We weren't going to be late, but I only said, "It won't matter, Montrose is always late anyway." I hoped that throwing her the memory of delicious Montrose might get her out of the mood her father's call had put her in.

"Right, right," she said, but the cloud over her followed us on the rest of the walk.

"Are you going to tell me what he said?" I asked as we made our way into the doors of Snyder Hall, where our class was five minutes from starting.

She looked closely at me. "That depends. I mean, I want to, Lily, I really do. But just where do your loyalties lie? Are you my friend first, or your father's spy?"

"I'm not his spy," I said, pissed.

She tilted her head at me, assessing. "Aren't you?"

"No," I said with more vehemence. "Screw it, I don't need to hear your secrets if you don't trust me," I said, walking past her into the building, taking a right and heading down the hallway to the lecture room.

"Okay, okay," Jane said when she sat down next to me in our regular seats. Syd was already there, her earbuds still in, though she nodded to me when I sat beside her.

Of course Montrose was late.

"He wants me to be a bridesmaid in Betsy's wedding at Christmastime."

"What the fuck?" Syd said, having heard only that as she took out her earbuds and turned her phone off.

"Exactly," Jane said to Syd, then looked at me with almost a challenge, like I'd be on her dad's side.

"How is that possible?" I asked. "I mean, forget that Betsy hates you—no offense."

She shrugged. "None taken."

"But you have to plan those things several months in advance. And I'm sure her wedding is probably going to be a big one."

"Monster."

"Then she'd have her bridesmaids asked and committed months ago." A look of guilt in Jane's eyes made me ask, "When exactly did Betsy ask you?"

"Oh, Betsy never asked me. Still hasn't. We don't speak. She totally hates me. But my dad's been bugging me about it for months."

"But Betsy must know, right? I mean, she can't just have an extra bridesmaid show up on the day of the wedding. Can she?"

I knew what magic tricks my father was capable of, and if he was anywhere near this—and now I had the sneaking suspicion he definitely was—then really, anything was possible.

"Who the hell knows? Between my father and yours, I'm thinking poor Betsy doesn't stand a chance of getting anything she wants—and that might include the groom."

"But to what end? I mean, what are they even up to after all these years? And what is having you being a bridesmaid going to achieve, other than being fodder for gossip?"

"I don't know. I can't figure that part out. Not evil-minded enough to think like those two Machiavellian fucks—"

"Good to hear you know your Florentine literature, Ms. Winters," Montrose said as he entered the room, throwing his messenger bag on the desk and moving to the lectern. "But I don't recall 'fucks' being part of Machiavelli's *The Prince*. Of course, if he were writing today, he might…No, he was never a lazy writer. Machiavelli? He'd come up with something better."

"Oh, come on," Jane said, leaning forward in her seat. "Surely there's always a place for a good fuck…in literature."

"An interesting theory. Maybe it should be the subject of your paper." He had already moved on from Jane, and she sat back in her seat.

The dark cloud around her only grew with Montrose not rising to her bait, and I knew that with her mood, and Lucas not calling, it was going to feel like an eternity before I saw Lucas at Andy's swim lesson tomorrow afternoon.

If he showed.

He showed.

He sat in the tile bleachers during the lesson, watching Andy. Each time I tried to meet his glance, he was looking at his brother, or one of the other kids, or somewhere else altogether.

It was one short week ago that I first saw him. When I was in this pool giving lessons and had felt like I was spiraling out of control just looking at him.

Now I had a feeling of absolute dread that I had lost him

before I ever even had him.

I wasn't even sure anybody could ever "have" Lucas Kade. That he would ever give his whole self to any girl. And from the way he wouldn't meet my eye, it seemed I wouldn't even get the chance to try.

He was wearing jeans, and this time it was a black Bribury T-shirt, not a polo. And, God, he was gorgeous.

I resolved to stop looking up at him. Though for most things I didn't want to be, I was in fact my father's daughter, and I tried to conjure up my father's obstinate pride.

If Lucas didn't want me…fuck him.

Oh God, but I wanted to fuck him. And have him fuck me.

But now it seemed he was just going to fuck me over.

"Lily, are you coming over for pizza tonight?" Andy asked as we were wrapping up and getting out of the pool.

"No, not tonight, Andy," I said, pushing his little body toward the locker room. "Go with Freddy now and I'll meet you on the other side."

Andy and my other little boy went with Freddy while I picked up his two girls and herded them through the showering process.

When I'd come through the locker room before the lessons, I'd noticed the steam room was cordoned off with sawhorses and yellow tape, almost like it was a crime scene.

It was. It was where Lucas stole my heart.

Ha! Melodramatic bullshit. I couldn't lose my heart to some ex-junkie townie in one week.

I immediately felt guilty and disloyal for those thoughts. It wasn't how I really thought of him; I was just trying to protect my heart, though I feared it was way too late for that.

I threw on my hoodie and yoga pants, kept my wet hair up in its bun, and made my way out to the hallway with my charges. The two girls Freddy taught moved over to his area. I waited for Andy to move to mine, but I couldn't find him.

"Didn't Andy come out with you?" I asked Freddy, ignoring Casey's mother, who wanted to speak with me about her kid.

"Yeah, he did. He left with his brother right away. The brother said he'd get any instructions on Andy's progress from you next time."

Freddy, of course, had seen me with Lucas and Andy on our Saturday swim date. Now Freddy was shooting me a sympathetic look. "He seemed to be in a hurry, like he had to be somewhere," he said, trying to be helpful.

He wasn't helpful. The whole situation sucked. And it was official.

Lucas was totally blowing me off.

THIRTEEN

❖

I COULDN'T believe I did it, but I swam extra laps that night and took a ton of time in the locker room. Yeah, I was waiting for him to show, though I told myself I wasn't.

Pathetic, and it didn't even work. He didn't show, and I wasn't about to stay all night to see if he'd resume work on the steam room tiling job.

I did skim under the tape to peek in. It looked like most of the demo work had been done, with all the old, gross tile gone. It looked bare and lonely and very sterile.

Kind of like how I felt.

On the walk home from the women's IM building, I resolved to shake this off, not let Lucas affect me this way. I was a hot freshman at an elite college, for Christ's sake; some townie blowing me off was not going to derail my college experience.

And yet I walked slowly, listening for a souped-up car to pull up behind me.

One never did.

Jane was on her phone, fighting with her father, when I came into the room. It amazed me how little Joseph Stratton knew his daughter. I'd only known Jane a little over a month and I knew that she would indeed rather transfer to a community college, or work her way through college entirely on her own, than do that which she said she wouldn't.

Jane would not make a good politician—absolutely no compromise in her.

Wanting to give Jane some privacy, though she motioned that it wasn't necessary, I threw my backpack on my bed and made my way through our bathroom to the other side of our suite to see if Syd was around.

When we first moved in, Syd shared a room with Megan, a girl from Nebraska, also here on scholarship. Megan seemed all right, and we tried to include her in stuff, but after the first two weeks her mother died and she left school to go home to Nebraska. She said she was coming back, and the residence association didn't put anyone else in with Syd, but we weren't betting on Megan returning anytime soon.

She'd taken all her stuff and Syd now lived in a room that was completely decked out on one side and totally empty on the other. Jane had said Syd should spread her stuff out, but Syd said she'd feel weird if Megan just showed up and Syd had squatted all over her area.

At the very least, Jane had put a sheet, a blanket, and a pillow on Megan's empty bed so we'd have somewhere to veg when we came over to Syd's side of the suite.

Which is what I did now, flopping down on the bed opposite Syd where she was propped up, textbook open on her lap.

"Hey," she said, pushing the book off her lap, curling her legs underneath her.

"Hey. I can leave if you want to study."

She shook her head. "It's okay. I need a break anyway."

I toed my kicks off and curled up on my side, adjusting the pillow under my head.

"So, what did he have to say about not calling you Sunday or Monday? A good excuse, at least? Did you let him have it before you kissed and made up?" She was smiling, not at all thinking that the situation was unresolved.

"None of the above. He took Andy and left before I even got out of the locker room. I never even talked to him." Stupid voice, cracking as I said the last.

"Oh, shit," Syd said, getting off her bed and crossing the small room to sit next to me. She placed a warm hand on my back, rubbing it. "Sorry, Lily, that sucks."

On some level I was glad Jane had been on the phone and that Syd was available. Jane would not have the sympathy and comfort Syd did. Which is surprising, since Syd is a pretty tough chick herself.

"Yeah," I said, "it does kind of suck."

"Of course it does," she said, now rubbing her hand up and down my back in a motion that made me really miss my mother.

"What a douche," she added, reminding me nothing of my mother.

"But that's the thing," I said, sitting up, crossing my legs, and facing Syd. "I don't think he is…a douche."

"Is your barometer trustworthy?"

I shrugged. "I don't know anymore. I always thought so." I had always been pretty dead-on with the guys I'd dated in the past. I knew which ones had the potential for jerkery, and was proven right most times. I also seemed to sense truly good guys, and had not been proven wrong on that front yet.

But maybe Lucas was my first major misread.

I shrugged again. "Who knows? I guess Schoolport douches read differently on my barometer than the Maryland ones I'm used to." I smiled, trying to make light of my words.

Syd went along with the facade. "Well, I can't speak for the Schoolport locals, not having met them, but I *know* the Bribury boys' douchery is much more polished than that of the guys in Queens. Maybe you just need to recalibrate your mechanism?"

"Yeah, maybe."

She pushed herself from the bed and went to her desk and picked up her phone. "Let's put some feelers out for the best parties this weekend. You just need one good hookup to get your mind off this guy." I didn't ask whom she was texting. Syd had networked a lot more than I had during our time at Bribury.

I let her do her thing, and didn't disagree with her, though I didn't have much faith in what she said.

I slept in the next morning, not having Montrose's class until eleven. I skipped going to the caf for breakfast with Jane, just having an apple and a cup of coffee from the room.

I considered blowing off class altogether, but that felt like self-pity and I didn't want to give Lucas that much power over my actions.

As I left the dorm, I heard, "Lily?" from a voice that zoomed through my body, sending sparks of awareness and self-protection.

Lucas stood to the side of the doors, leaning against one of the pillars that held up the overhang. He had his phone out, his fingers poised, as if he stopped mid-text when he saw me.

"I was just texting you," he said.

"Why?" I said. There must have been more anger in my voice than I realized, given the way Lucas's eyes widened.

"I...I was hoping we could talk."

"What about?" Less anger this time, more curiosity.

"I just wanted to explain why I haven't called or texted."

"I'm on my way to class."

He nodded, stepping away from the pillar, walking slowly toward me. "Yeah, sure. I get that. Maybe later."

Sometimes you have moments when you just *know* you're at a fork in the road. That whatever you say or do next will decide something major in your life. Maybe I was being too dramatic, but I just *knew* that if I didn't talk with Lucas right now, there would be no hope for us.

The real question was: did I want there to be hope for us?

"I can skip class," I said. "My room's empty, let's go up there."

"Really?" he asked. I gave one small nod, then turned and returned into the dorm, Lucas at my side.

We rode the elevator up to the third floor in silence, but he stood very close to me. When we exited the elevator and I turned to the right, Lucas took my hand and held it as we made our way down the hall. It was warm and rough and damn, but it felt so right.

I unlocked the door and stood back, letting Lucas enter the room first. He did, taking his time and looking around. I tried to see it through his eyes—a blending of two very different styles that seemed to work. Jane's side was eclectic and edgy, and yet kind of peaceful in a way. She had framed black-and-white photography on the walls, though sparingly. Her bedding was white with a black pattern through it, and some bright red as well. Her pillows and throw blanket were in the bright red, but her desk accessories were a deep eggplant. It was jarring when you looked at it at first, but then it all kind of blended together nicely once you got used to it.

Kind of like Jane.

My side was a study in comfortable textures and soothing colors. My comforter was a gorgeous sea foam color with white accents. A slate-gray cashmere throw lay at the foot of my bed.

My mother and I had gone shopping together to pick out all my stuff, then had a nice lunch at the mall. Over burgers, we'd talked about the great find of the comforter and how nice my room would look. How excited she was for me to be starting school. She'd even told some stories about her and my dad in college together, a wistful yet tender look in her eye. A look I didn't often see in my typically all-business mother.

It'd been a really good day.

I didn't have much on my walls. I hadn't wanted to bring the posters of the bands I liked that adorned the walls of my bedroom at home. I thought that might be too, you know, high school.

And I hadn't wanted to put a ton of family photos on the walls, either. I'd wanted to start fresh, be a new person. Wasn't that the whole idea?

The problem was, I didn't know who I wanted to be. Who was Lily Spaulding if not Grayson and Susan Spaulding's daughter? If not Alexis's younger or Gray's older sister?

Was I, like most of my wall space, bare?

Was Lucas my definition? Was loving Lucas who I was to

become?

Saturday night, I would have said an overwhelming yes. Today, I didn't think so.

Though, standing behind him, watching his long hair move from side to side as he took in the whole room…

"I'm glad you came," I said in almost a whisper. It was more to myself, but his back stiffened, and his head gave a small nod.

I locked the door behind me. "Let me just text Jane that I'm not coming to class so she doesn't worry." I pulled out my phone and quickly did the deed.

Skipping class, I texted.

You need to get your ass out of bed and stop obsessing about that loser, she responded.

Lucas here now. We're going to talk.

A pause. Either Montrose had just come in and she'd had to put her phone away, or for once Jane was speechless. Textless?

Make the SOB grovel first.

First? She seemed to know there'd be a second act to this visit.

Lucas crossed to my side of the room and sat down on my bed, then turned to watch me. He was wearing jeans and a black hoodie. So simple, yet he looked so good. And seeing his large body taking up most of my small bed…

Yes, there would be an act two today.

I set my phone down on my dresser and put my backpack on the floor next to it. "How did you know what side was mine?" I asked as I went to the desk chair and sat down.

Our desks were side by side along the wall that separated our beds. Oftentimes while studying at the desk, I would turn the swivel desk chair and put my feet up on my bed, they were that close. I didn't do that now, just kept my legs down, feet on the carpeted floor.

Yes, we had paid the extra for the carpeted floor. And we had a Keurig, and a small fridge, and a large TV, though not nearly as big as the one at Lucas's apartment. Gorgeous leather office chairs replaced the stiff wooden ones that we'd been issued. We'd had the guy who builds lofts create cool overhead storage units that helped with the small closet space.

My father didn't want to get caught pulling strings to get Jane and me into an Ivy League school ("The press would have a field day with that"), but he had no problem with me living in the style he felt becoming to a Spaulding. And so, our room was decked out way more than most college freshman's rooms. Though, honestly, it wasn't that much different than the other rooms here at Bribury.

"I don't know Jane that well," Lucas said, "But I know you, Lily. And I knew what side of the room was yours the moment I walked in."

I didn't know whether that was a good thing or that I was predictably boring, with none of Jane's flair and edge. But I let it go; there were more important things to deal with today. Like... "So, why are you here, Lucas?"

I expected him to start throwing out typical guy excuses about being really busy and meaning to call, and he could throw in some good "Andy needing him" stuff to make it even more legit.

"I really don't know," he said. He leaned forward, resting his forearms on his thighs, clasping his hands together. It was the same pose he'd been sitting in when I first saw him at the pool, way up in the stands, watching Andy. Watching me.

My heart clenched tight, but I told it to settle down. We needed answers, my heart and I, and I couldn't let it run the show. "What does that mean?" I said, trying to sound indifferent, when I was anything but.

He bowed his head, looking at his hands. His hair swung forward and I literally sat on my hands so I wouldn't reach out and push it back and away from his face.

"It means I really don't know why I'm here, Lily. I know I messed up by not calling or texting, and of course I did that on purpose. And then yesterday, seeing you at the pool..." He looked up, and the pain in his brown eyes matched the pain I so desperately felt but so desperately wanted to hide.

"And then you left with Andy," I reminded him.

"Yeah. Dick move, I know that. It was all a dick move, everything from Sunday on. And who knows—maybe coming here today is the biggest dick move of them all. Maybe I should just leave you in peace."

This. This was the moment I needed to decide whether I wanted Lucas Kade in my life or not. A simple "I think that would be best," and he'd leave, I knew it.

I did not want to be the girl who was perpetually played by a guy who treated her poorly, then let him back into her life with a few prettily done mea culpas. I *so* did not want to be that girl.

And yet, when he looked at me, waiting for me to speak, all I could say was, "I want you to stay."

His shoulders eased and I realized how tense they'd been. My body eased as well, but we weren't quite there yet.

"So, why don't you tell me what's going on. Why all the shitty treatment, then showing up now?"

He relaxed a bit, settled in as if for a long story. He leaned back, putting his hands on the bed behind him. The plushness of my comforter seemed to swallow them up, and from my chair it looked like his arms just disappeared into the sea. He stretched out his legs, crossing his feet. If I turned just a tiny bit, my feet would brush his, they were so close. But I stayed where I was, waiting.

"Sunday morning, when Andy woke up, he asked what we were going to do that day," he began. I nodded. It sounded like what any six-year-old boy would say.

"No, I mean, he asked what *we* were going to do. Him, me, and you."

"Oh," I said.

"Yeah, exactly. And you know what? My first thought was, *Let's call Lily and see what we are going to do today.*"

"But you didn't call," I said, though of course he knew that.

He stared at me for a moment, his eyes searching mine. Then

he broke contact, looking at his worn work boots. "No, I didn't call. And I caught myself and didn't say any of that to Andy. But God, I wanted to call, Lily. I wanted nothing more than to spend another day with you...and Andy."

I waited, so still, not moving an inch. I thought about lying around with a hung-over Jane all day Sunday when instead I could have been with Lucas.

"But then, what?" he asked. "So we spend Sunday together. What? Like some family or something? You're a college freshman. You just got out of your family unit. You're supposed to be out partying and meeting new people. Not discussing the developmental growth of some townie's kid brother."

"I care about Andy."

He looked back up at me. "I know you do. And I don't want to take advantage of that. If it were just me? Well, it would still be selfish to ask you to hang with me instead of your new friends, but I'd do it."

His voice dropped almost to a whisper, almost to a growl when he said "I'd do it," and my heart, already racing from the moment I'd seen Lucas downstairs, started beating even faster.

"I'd do it in a heartbeat," he said, and I wondered if he could hear mine. "But it's not just me. And I honestly don't know how long I'm going to be doing daddy duty with Andy."

"I could—" He held up a hand, stalling my words. Which was just as well. I wasn't certain what I was going to say.

"And to be honest, I hope it *is* for a long time. I *like* being with Andy. It's good for me, and I hope it's good for him. I know it's better for him to have my mom, when she's...healthy. But, we're not really sure when that's going to be, or for how long."

"So you think it's permanent?"

He shrugged, then returned his hand to the sea. "I'm trying to find a cheap lawyer to discuss my options. CPS has been really good about me being with him, him staying in the home and all that. But I want to know what the options are, long term, in case my mom isn't...capable."

"What's CPS?"

"Child Protective Services. See? That you don't know that totally symbolizes what I'm trying to say. We—our situation—are totally out of your world right now. Hell, most likely you'd go through your whole life and not need to know what CPS stands for. Me? I knew it when I was five."

"I agree, I'm not ready to play stepmommy to a first grader, but I do like kids. And I like Andy a lot. I mean, I teach kids' swimming lessons. I was a lifeguard at the club pool the last two summers. I *like* kids."

I didn't mention that I did the lessons so it would look good on my résumé, and that I lifeguarded mainly for the great tan. It wasn't a lie. Andy was a cool kid and I wouldn't mind spending time with him and Lucas.

But Lucas was also right—it was more than I had bargained for when I got into the back seat of Stick's car that night.

God, that night seemed like months ago, not just last week.

"You took the choice away from me," I said to Lucas.

"Yes," he said, no guilt in his voice.

"Look, I don't want to confuse Andy any more than he probably is with all that's going on. And I know between him and working the shift you do, you've got a lot going on."

"Yes?"

I took a deep breath. I could be going out on a very thin limb here, but the fact that Lucas had shown up here this morning gave me the courage to slowly ease my way onto it.

"But we could still find time for just you and me to...hang out."

A small, tentative smile played across his face, then died. "It'd be at weird times. And occasionally we'd do stuff with Andy. And I would totally understand when you wanted to do stuff with your friends." A cloud of uncertainty passed through his eyes. "I'll try not to be a dick about it—when I know you're going out and I'm at home with Andy. But..."

I didn't say it, but I knew I'd rather be with Lucas at his small apartment, even with Andy sleeping in the next room, than at a kegger with Jane and Syd, trying to get with some guy for the night. I couldn't imagine wanting to hook up with anyone else when I knew Lucas was just across town.

I kept quiet on all that, of course. I'm not stupid. I wasn't going to give Lucas any more ammunition than he already had to stomp on my heart.

Speaking of which…"So, the dick move of not calling me? And blowing me off yesterday?"

He held up his hands in surrender. "Never again. I thought I was doing what was best for you. For all of us. But yeah, I screwed that up."

"Big time."

"Yeah, I know. I thought it would be easier to just shut it down before it got out of hand. When I saw you yesterday, with Andy, it just kind of reinforced to me that the kid thing was a part-time gig for you, a couple of afternoons a week. That's all it *should* be for you."

"So you bailed."

"Yeah. Like I said, dick move, and it won't happen again."

"What happens the next time we hit a rough patch? Or you get twitchy and start thinking about what you think is best for me."

"Umm…"

"We talk it out," I finished for him.

He smiled, a wide, genuine smile that made my breath catch in my chest. So, so gorgeous when he smiled. "Stick's more of the talker. I just sit there and look pretty." His grin was infectious, and I smiled back at him.

"Well, pretty as you are, you're going to have to talk to me. You blow me off like that again, and that's the last you'll see of me." I was still smiling, and my voice had a joking, teasing tone to it. But he knew I meant it.

His smile faded a little. "I know. And Lily, I'm really sorry that I handled it so badly. This is kind of new for me."

That stopped me. Gorgeous Lucas, football star Lucas, must have had tons of girls coming on to him.

"What, exactly, is new to you?"

He waved a hand between us. "This. Us. You. Being… caring…about how a girl's feeling."

"You didn't care about other girls' feelings?" Maybe my radar about Lucas being a good guy really was off.

"Well, yeah, sure. But there was never any girl that I went out of the way to… Listen, I'm not great with words, and I know I'm going to screw up what I want to say."

"You're right. I don't want to talk about other girls in your life."

"That's just it. That's what I'm trying to say…badly. There were no other girls where I felt like this. Wondering where they were, what they were doing. And not in a stalker kind of way. But because I really cared where you were, what you were thinking, what you were feeling. It's all different with you, Lily, and…and…I don't really know what I'm doing." He sat forward, his arms once again resting on his knees. But this was not a relaxed pose; he was leaning toward me. He put a hand out as if to touch my knee, then pulled it back. "So, bear with me, okay?" he whispered.

"Okay," I whispered back, with no hesitation.

I would bear with Lucas. And, I suspected, very shortly be bare with him, too.

FOURTEEN

HE MOVED to the edge of the bed, then dropped to his knees on the floor in front of me. He placed his hands carefully on my knees, gently, as if I might bolt with a sudden movement.

I wasn't going anywhere.

I placed my hands on top of his. He turned his up so we were palm to palm.

"Remember what I said to you that first night? Right outside this building?" he said, looking up at me.

I did and nodded, but I waited, wanting him to repeat it. Wanted him to deny it, take it back.

"I'm not what you need," he said, echoing his own words.

I hadn't answered him that night, but now I said, "Don't I get to decide what I need?"

"And do you? Do you need…this? Us? Me? God, I want to be. I want to be what you need." Pulling his hands from under mine, he wedged them between the back of my knees and the chair, rolling it closer to him. I instinctively spread my legs so that the chair slid right against his chest.

"Yes," I whispered.

"Yes, what?" he said, his voice low and throaty.

Excitement rushed through me. My body, tingling since I'd seen him, moved to fever pitch.

"I need…us." I slid to the edge of the chair, my legs dangling down at his sides. My ballet flats fell off my feet with a subtle movement. I heard them plunk softly on the carpeting like the sound was a million miles away. Everything was a million miles away, except Lucas right in front of me.

"I need…to kiss you," I said. I wasn't sure if I moved off the chair first, or he pulled me, but I was straddling his lap, my hands in his hair and my mouth on his.

He tasted like sweet coffee and I drove my tongue into his mouth, nearly frenzied with wanting to taste him.

He sensed my urgency, and wrapped his arms tightly around me, his hands going to my hair. In seconds, he had released my bun. I moved away from the kiss, his face following mine. He opened dazed eyes, watching to see if I had changed my mind.

No way in hell had I changed my mind. I wanted Lucas with an intensity I'd never felt before.

It was like a physical craving, like when you needed salty chips or chocolate. It was what had always been missing with other guys I dated. It had definitely been missing with the one boyfriend I'd slept with.

Craving. I craved Lucas. Probably like he had craved Oxy.

Who knows, it might be just as dangerous.

I took my hands from his silky tresses and ran my fingers through my own loose hair, lifting it, playing with it. Like some skanky pole dancer, but Lucas's eyes grew wider and the bulge that I sat on grew bigger. Taking the stripper analogy a bit further, I ground on him, saying a silent thank-you for the thin fabric of my leggings.

He hissed, "Jesus Christ, Lily," then his mouth was devouring mine again. He grabbed both my hands in one of his and lowered them from my hair, but kept them behind my back. Like he was arresting me or something.

He moved back to rest on his haunches, taking me with him, the contact now even more direct. I ground harder, needing so much more of him.

"I know, baby," he whispered. "We'll get there. I promise." Then he kept on kissing me.

I wanted my hands free to touch his magnificent body. But I also liked being held back like this, having no control. Because that was how I'd felt from the moment I first saw Lucas—that I wasn't in control of my own feelings. And certainly not in control of my body.

"Lucas," I moaned into his mouth. "I need…"

He tipped me, brought me down onto my back on the floor, releasing my arms as he did, and following me to the carpet. My legs spread wide for him, giving him the space to be where I needed him.

My hands free, I reached for his hoodie, pulling, yanking. He chuckled at my urgency, sitting up between my legs and—too damn leisurely—pulling the hoodie up and over his head, tossing it across the floor. "The T-shirt too," I said as I unzipped and peeled off my fleece jacket. I pulled my sweater off, wriggling out of it while I still lay on the floor beneath him. I was happy to see that I'd put on one of my prettier bras this morning—lavender satin with pretty lace along the upper edges of the cups. Cups that were becoming increasingly confining as my breasts began to ache for his touch.

His long torso loomed over me and I just stared at him for a moment, admiring.

"What?" he said.

I shook my head with the tiniest of motions. "Nothing. I just like looking at you."

He grimaced at my words, but in a cute, kind of embarrassed way. "Please," he said. "You're the one who's a fucking work of art." He ran the back of his hand from the bottom of my bra down my tummy, skimming the waistband of my leggings.

I could watch him watch me forever. But I needed to touch him. "Come here," I breathed softly, waiting for him to lean over me, which he did, his strong arms bracketing my head, his hands dug into the carpet, next to my hair, some of it entangling with his fingers.

I snaked one hand along his bicep, like the twining ivy tattoo, wrapping my arm around his. My other hand slid up his abs to his chest, the reverse of what he'd just done to me.

He held himself away from me, still above, but within touching distance, which I took full advantage of. His chest was muscled, like the rest of him, and his skin was warm and smooth and rough at the same time.

He reached behind me and I eased off the carpet enough for him to unhook my bra and peel it off. As he untangled the straps from my arms, I flopped them back on the floor, over my head.

I wasn't one who typically reveled in my nakedness with boys, but I wanted Lucas to see me. Wanted to watch his lids grow heavy and lick his lips, as he did now. I arched my back slightly, offering myself to him.

"Lily," he whispered before he lowered his mouth to my breast. His hand kneaded and played with the other one, and the sensation was so intense I almost screamed. I didn't, though I did moan his name.

"Yes," he growled, then returned to sucking on me, licking and teasing my pebbling nipple.

I wrapped one arm around his broad shoulders, holding him to me, never wanting him anywhere else, doing anything other than what he was doing to my body. My other hand lodged in his hair, lifting and tunneling through the silky mass.

He moved to my other breast, and the sun coming through the window above the desk reflected on the wetness he left behind, making me glisten and sparkle. It matched the feelings he brought out in me.

His hand covered my wet breast, pinching and pulling the nipple as I squirmed underneath him.

His hips started rocking into me, the denim of his jeans creating a sweet friction against my leggings. "More," I whispered, spreading my legs even wider, cursing the barrier of cloth between us, yet not wanting him to move from what he was doing, even to take our clothes off.

"This," he answered. "This, this, this," he said, kissing my breasts so sweetly between each word that he spoke. His hair fell like a curtain over his face, over my chest, swinging as he moved from breast to breast. I could see snatches of my aching flesh and his wet mouth through the dark, glossy hair as he feasted on me.

He was rocking faster against me, and I could feel the wetness seeping from me, wanting relief. "Lucas, please," I moaned as I thrust my hips up to meet his.

He didn't acknowledge my words, but his mouth moved down my body, kissing and licking my tummy, dipping his tongue into my navel, causing a bolt of desire to rocket through me.

I was really restless under him now, my legs trying to wrap around him, trying to find relief as he ground himself into me. But I knew I'd get no relief—not the relief I really needed—until Lucas was deep inside me.

He must have felt it too, because he lifted himself away from me and sat up on his haunches. Before I could groan about the loss of his body on mine, he was peeling my leggings down, lifting and moving each of my legs, one at a time, to get the stretchy material off of me. He flung it over my head, beyond me, to Jane's side of the room.

He placed his big hands on my hips, his thumbs right at the elastic waist of my lavender satin panties. It was a sheer luck that my panties matched my bra, and though the bra was long gone, I said a silent prayer of thanks to the underwear gods. Not that it would have mattered to Lucas if I'd been wearing big, ugly granny panties, if the way he was hungrily staring at my body was any indication.

He began to slide his thumbs under the elastic, to take the panties off, then stopped. Instead, he rocked back on his heels and effortlessly lifted himself from the floor and stood over me.

"What?" I asked, starting to scramble up, my legs catching in his.

"No. Don't move," he said. I stopped, and instead stayed where I was, but slightly propped up on my elbows.

He leaned over and untied his work boots and pulled them

off, his socks following. Setting them to the side of the bed, he stood back up and ran a hand down his chest, like I had done. But where I had stopped, he continued, cupping himself, stroking along the outside of jeans, outlining his large erection.

I let out a sigh, not meaning to, but he smiled a very-sure-of-himself smile. And why not? The guy was gorgeous.

And he was mine.

He unzipped his jeans while his eyes roamed over my body, his smile fading from cocksure to feral. Sliding his jeans off in one motion, he stepped out of them, then bent over to pick them up, grabbing his wallet out of the back pocket. He pulled a condom out and dropped it to the floor, landing next to my hip. Then his eyes met mine, burned into me. I licked my lips in anticipation and I could see his nostrils flare in arousal. He pulled out another condom and dropped that one so it landed right on top of my panties. Then he tossed the jeans over my chair and sank down to his knees, dressed only in black boxer briefs.

I put my feet on the back of his calves, rubbing against his strong legs, lifting my hips up to him. He placed his hands back on my hips, thumbs spread wide over me, almost touching the condom that lay between them. Breathing deeply, I was almost suffocated by the feeling of contentment—the *rightness*—of this moment. "Lucas...I..." I couldn't say more, though I certainly felt more.

But he knew, like he seemed to know every feeling I had, if only because he had them too.

"Me too," he said quietly, though he was agreeing to something unspoken.

And that was enough for now.

I reached for the waistband of his briefs, pulling them down, freeing him. Wrapping my fingers around the hard girth of his erection, I began slowly stroking. He let out a hiss and I squeezed.

"Christ, Lily, you're killing me," he ground out between gritted teeth. His head was thrown back, his hair dangling down his neck, and I was amazed at the rush of emotion—the deep,

deep emotion—that welled up inside of me.

Lust and hunger, yes, but I knew that was just the tip of the iceberg of what I felt for Lucas Kade.

I squeezed him again and ran my thumb over his head, feeling the moisture. I ran my nail, ever so lightly, along the underside of the head of his cock, wanting him to be at the fever pitch I was.

It worked. Another strong hiss, and a "fuck," and he was on me. Kissing me senseless, his tongue darting into my mouth, sucking on mine. His hands fumbled for the condom that rested on my panties and, as he snatched it up, he ground the back of his hand into my mound.

"God," I groaned. "Hurry."

He had the condom on in no time, and I chose not to think about how practiced, how familiar, those movements seemed to him.

As if he couldn't even wait to pull my panties off, he pushed the elastic to one side and ran a finger up my wet slit.

"Jesus, Lily. So wet for me." His words, in a throaty voice hoarse with passion, made me even wetter, and he grunted in satisfaction.

Yanking my panties further to the side, he slid a finger into me and I jerked in response, my body clenching around him.

"So tight, so ready. You're ready for me, aren't you?"

I nodded, barely able to speak. I breathed out a "yes" with my sigh, as he added another finger and began stroking me. I brought my hands up to his ass, pulling his briefs further down so I could feel his skin. His glutes clenched as I molded my hands around them, urging him closer.

"Lucas, I need you inside me," I said, pulling on his tight ass.

"I am inside you," he teased, turning his fingers up in the most delicious way as he continued to stroke.

I dug my nails into his ass in response and he laughed, albeit a tight, strangled laugh.

"Not my sweet, quiet Lily after all, are you?" he teased as he bent his head and sucked on my breast again, his fingers stroking faster now. "Do it again," he said, then returned to sucking on my nipple.

I squeezed his ass again, my nails digging deeper. He bit my nipple and I moaned his name, needing the frenzy to stop, certain I would die if it didn't. Certain I would die if it did.

"There's a little bit of dirty girl in you, isn't there, Lily?" He looked up then, his mouth away from my breast, his eyes looking deep into mine. "I knew it when I first saw you. When you let Andy go under because you were looking at me. You're sweet and nice, but there's a streak of steel in you that nobody sees. Hell, maybe you haven't even seen it yet. And the passion? The passion that you're either afraid to unleash, or no one's ever tried to free it before."

I felt like he saw through to my very soul, like he knew more about me than I even knew myself. And yet I sensed he was right. I had never been challenged, never had to define myself. And I had never—not even close—felt the kind of roaring passion in my body that I did now.

"No one's ever freed it," I answered him, even as I was figuring it out myself.

He smiled, like he was almost proud of me. Then the smile turned dangerous and he said, "I will. I'm going to free all of that rolling around inside you Lily. And it will be mine."

I drenched his fingers that were still inside me, and with one more strategic curve and stroke of those magic digits, I burst apart, shuddering and clenching. I closed my eyes, enjoying the shattering lights that burst in my head.

"Open your eyes," he commanded, and I quickly obeyed. The spasms were still rolling through me, his fingers still playing. I could see my breasts shaking with each jerk, and Lucas's eyes feasted on the movement. Sitting back on his heels, he pulled his fingers from me and wrapped both of his hands around the back of my thighs, pulling me high up onto his legs, my ass sitting on his thighs, my legs spread wide in front of his hard cock. He still didn't remove my panties, just slid them over, wet as they were, and guided his cock to me.

I could have told him I was on the pill and he didn't need a condom. But that would have started the discussion about pasts, and I didn't want to have that, not yet. I wanted to imagine there was no girl before me for Lucas. Because, even though I wasn't a virgin, and had had semi-regular sex with my boyfriend my senior year, it felt like Lucas was my first.

Besides, it was better to be extra safe, and so I was happy to have Lucas wear the condom.

He slid deep inside me, filling me up much more than his fingers had, fitting me to him.

"Fuck, you feel so good," he whispered, holding still, taking in the sense of our oneness. I tightened around him, wanting him deeper, wanting him to seep into my bones, into my soul.

"Lily," he whispered, as if he knew what I felt, how close I needed him to be. He began to move slowly, the glide of him inside me luxurious and decadent.

He smelled like soap and laundry detergent, fresh and clean, no cologne, nothing to get in the way of...him. And arousal. I could smell the arousal on him as surely as he did mine. His skin was glistening in the sun with a fine sheen of sweat from holding back.

"Let go," I said, and he knew what I meant. His hips bore down into me. At the angle he had me, I couldn't reach him unless I sat up, and I was loving the feel of him over me, so I just spread my arms out over my head on the floor. The carpet was soft and dense beneath my back, and I dug my fingers into the plush fiber as Lucas began pounding into me. He sat up a bit, getting better leverage with his knees, and now my breasts were bouncing madly with each drive that he made.

"Hold them," he grunted, and I didn't have to ask what he meant. I grasped my tits, wishing they were Lucas's hands. But his hands were busy gripping my hips as he plunged deeper and deeper into me.

I played with my nipples as he had, and it felt good, but

not as good as his mouth had. "Pinch them," he said. I did, and I moaned as he hit a lovely spot deep inside me. "Yes, keep doing that. Keep clenching your pussy too. Bear down on me, Lily."

I did, summoning all my inner strength as he began pumping in a staccato rhythm that played like a beat in my head.

One of his hands slid from my hip under the panties to join his pistoning cock. He thumbed my clit, sliding and circling.

"Come again, Lily. Come again for me while I'm deep inside you." His thumb rubbed around, wiggling, and I exploded, clenching and shaking around him.

"Yeah, that's it," he growled, his words barely decipherable between the roaring in my head, and his throaty voice. He tensed, and pumped again, releasing into me. Shoulders tensed, those amazing biceps flexed, he continued to stroke. The thumb eased from my clit, slid up my panties, leaving a trail of wetness on the satin. His hands eased on my hips, clasping me gently as he pushed a few last strokes inside me.

My breathing started to return to normal, making me notice just how erratic it had become.

My hands released my breasts, dropping to the floor at my sides. Spent, depleted, and oh so satisfied.

Lucas pulled out of me, and lay down next to me on his side, his hand on my tummy, just below my still-heaving breasts. He propped himself up on an elbow, looking down at me, running his hand all over me, sending shots of electricity all though my already electrified body.

I ran a leg up one of his shins and he startled a bit when I hit his knee. We both looked down and saw the beginning redness of what would most likely be a rug burn on his knees.

"I'll probably have one on my back," I joked, and we both smiled.

He leaned down and softly kissed me. A few more sweet kisses, then one long, deep one. When he raised his head, he said, "Then we'll have to move it to the bed for round two."

Still a pile of Jell-O from round one, I couldn't wait.

FIFTEEN

❖

Lucas

> *I didn't believe in second chances.*
> *And then I took a chance on Lily Spaulding.*

I WATCHED Lily as she slept. I sat in the office chair a few feet away from her. I needed to distance myself at least just a little bit. I knew it wouldn't be for long—I just couldn't seem to stay away from Lily. And after the past three days, I just didn't want to even try anymore.

It had been pure torture not calling or texting her, but in some fucked-up way I thought I was doing her a favor. Yeah, right. Only a favor if I really did stay away from her. And I now knew that wasn't gonna happen.

The pull was too strong. Had been from the first time I saw her in the pool with Andy.

She stretched on the bed and I held my breath. The movement—every move she made—held me in thrall.

I didn't really understand it. I've been with good-looking girls before. Shit, they hung all over me in high school and at USC because of the football thing. Even now, when I was nothing but a fucking janitor with a six-year-old to take care of, I had no shortage of offers.

And crazy as it sounded, I didn't want to be with anyone else now that Lily was giving me the time of day.

There was no reason for her to do so. As I told her that first night, there was no way in hell I was what she needed.

But she said she was willing to give it a try, Andy and my sucky work schedule and all, so I was going to give it my best shot. Something I wasn't willing to do before—it hadn't even crossed my mind.

And no more dick moves.

She stretched again, raising an arm above her head, but slept on. It looked like a swimming stroke, one that was as natural and graceful on her in bed as it was when she cut through the water. Her arm was toned, and still had remnants of a tan. It nestled into her white sheets surrounded by this blanket that reminded me of the ocean. In fact, the whole thing looked like a sexy-as-hell wave riding on the sea. Her ass was like a crest of a wave, white and stark against the rest of her tanned body. Which kind of looked like sand dunes rising out of the ocean if I squinted.

A thought—a vision—sprang to mind, and I looked around Lily's desk for paper and something to write with. I grabbed a legal pad and pen and stared at Lily again for a few minutes, happy just to watch her.

Christ, when was the last time I'd felt this…yeah, okay, happy?

I blurred my vision a bit, wanting to capture the whole, which was impossible, because my eyes kept coming back to her face, nestled in the sheets. Her black hair covered most of it, and ran down her bare back, almost to her spectacular ass. In silhouette, it almost appeared like the black of night hovering over dunes, with the white of the sheets being waves that rose from the ocean and broke against the sand of her skin.

I drew the lines and angles. Not really sketching, I sucked at that, but capturing the places body and sand and sea met and collided. I had an idea for the steam room and I didn't want to forget how Lily's body rose out of the ocean of her blanket.

Not that I was likely to forget her body. Or this day. Being inside Lily, driving into her as her body opened up to me—craved me—was far and away the best sex I'd ever had. And I'd been with girls—women—with a lot more experience than Lily.

But that was what it boiled down to—it wasn't just sex with Lily. I could get that anywhere. And it wouldn't be nearly the hassle as finding time for Lily, and getting to her on the other side of town, and all those fucking feelings of inadequacy that I had when I was around her.

Lily was a hell of a lot more than just sex to me, and that had scared the shit out of me on Sunday.

It still did, to be truthful. But now? Now it was worth being scared shitless all the time. Time to man up and deal with these all-over-the-place feelings I'd had since I first saw how good she was with those little kids.

That night with Stick and Jane in the car, when Stick had given the definition of that stupid Bribury Basics name? I knew Lily was thinking she fit it to a tee. And maybe on the surface she did.

But there was more to Lily. She wasn't a Basic, no matter how many North Face pullovers she had in her closet.

I saw it right away, that first day in the pool.

The thing was, I wasn't so sure that she saw it.

"What are you doing?" she said, startling me from my notes/drawing. Her voice was drowsy and full of…seduction. Though I don't think she was being all sexy-voiced on purpose. That's just what an afternoon of spectacular banging did to her. I smiled at my own stupidity (thank God unspoken), and she smiled back at me.

Holy Christ, when she smiled at me, it was like all the bad shit that had happened lately just fell away.

"Just jotting down some notes for the steam room job," I said, ripping the paper off the tablet, folding it, and putting it in the back pocket of my jeans.

For our second round, I'd lifted Lily from the floor and moved us both to the small bed, pushing the covers aside so I could see her gorgeous body against stark white sheets. I'd been hard again in an instant, but we'd taken our time, kissing and touching and feeling more than we had that frenzied first coupling.

Now I sat in just my jeans, and even though I'd come like a motherfucker two times in the last three hours, her smile made me hard again in an instant. I was mentally doing the math of how late I could be to pick up Andy and how quickly I could get inside her, when she asked, "How did you become a tile guy, anyway? Or is this your first time doing it?"

The memories of how I learned to tile quickly went from fond and sweet to painful, and my fledgling hard-on subsided.

"I've known how to do it since I was a kid. But this is the first time I'm doing it as a major project on my own." I patted my back pocket, where I'd placed my squiggles of her body as inspiration. "That's why I want to do an extra-good job. Hopefully it will lead to more tiling jobs around campus and less…towel boy." I grinned at her, remembering her standing in nothing but a towel that first day in the locker room.

"You're a *very* good towel boy," she said with a bit of sass. I liked it when she pulled out the sass. She didn't do it often, which made it all the more potent.

"Not that good. I didn't get the one towel I wanted," I reminded her.

She smiled, but said nothing more. Oh, right. I was supposed to be doing the talking.

"My dad was a tiling expert. Did the usual stuff, kitchens and baths, but did a ton of custom work too. He'd take me on jobs with him when they fell on the weekend and my mom was working. He'd have me swirl on the adhesive, showing me just the right amount, the right technique. He had a great eye for colors and designs that you might not think would work well together, but they did." I sat back in the chair, remembering.

I laid a hand on my bare stomach and noticed that Lily's eyes followed my movement. There was just a tiny movement from her legs, but I knew that she liked watching me, liked my body.

Which was only fair, because I was crazy about her long, lean—but just enough curves in the right places—body.

"And so he taught you? Your dad?" she asked, pulling my mind away from her body…as much as it ever could be.

"Yeah. Well, not really. I was just a kid, so it was more 'See what I'm doing here, Lucas' kind of stuff. Though he'd let me mix the grout up and things like that. But I watched. I…watched."

I still remembered his strong and beat-up hands as he'd apply the adhesive. The precision with which he'd place the tile, even for custom mosaic work. Work that looked like he was making it up as he went, though I now knew he must have seen it in his head. Most times he didn't even bother with the plastic dividers between tiles, so sure was he of his own skill at placing the ceramic and glass tiles.

"How old did you say you were when he died?"

"Twelve," I said with no hesitation. Cursing the near croak that came out in my voice. I couldn't look at Lily, didn't want to see any pity from her. Instead, I stared out the window, seeing the Bribury campus from a view I'd never seen before. Inside and high up. It was a beautiful, small campus. Hard to imagine there was such ugliness only a short car ride away.

"He worked very hard to make a good living. My mom worked hard too. We didn't have a lot, but he got us out of the worst neighborhoods. I mean, we weren't on the Bribury side of town…" I waved at the scene outside the window. She didn't say anything, and I silently thanked her. I didn't need to hear any rich-girl guilt about how she was sure we did the best we could or some such shit. But Lily didn't do that. She just waited. I could feel her eyes on me, but I kept my gaze out the window.

"So, yeah, we weren't in the worst neighborhood in town, but it was bad enough. My dad was shot during a convenience store robbery. Just in there to get a pack of cigarettes on his way home from work."

"Oh my God. Oh, Lucas, I'm so sorry." Still she did not move. Thankfully, or I probably wouldn't have been able to go on.

Would most likely be bawling like a baby against Lily's soft tits.

I nodded, acknowledging her words of sympathy. "Yeah, it was bad. It really threw my mom. She was basically catatonic for a year. She lost her job as a secretary here on campus, 'cause she just wouldn't show up. Later I realized she'd started…self-medicating, trying to block out the pain." I swallowed, the words hard to speak. Hard to think about that time in my life, but also because…

"That's what you did, too," she said, totally getting it. Totally getting me. "With the Oxy. Blocked out the pain. And not just from your shoulder."

No, not just my shoulder. It was the pain that I had lost my one chance at making a better life. That salvation, an easy life for my mom and Andy, had been in my grasp, with the likelihood of an NFL contract, when it all was just torn away, like the tendon in my shoulder.

"Yeah," I said softly, almost a whisper. There was no judgment in Lily's voice, but I still judged myself. And came up short every time.

But now, now it seemed I was getting a second chance to do it right. Oh, it might not be the money of the NFL, or the joy of watching my mom and Andy move into a swanky new place. But this? Taking care of Andy and seeing that my mom gets help? Working a good, honest job where I wasn't looking over my shoulder all the time? Knowing what money I made was paying the rent on Andy and my mom's place and not going straight to a dealer for more Oxy?

Yeah, I was not going to fuck up this second chance.

I looked at her then, finally able to handle what looking at a naked Lily would do to me in this vulnerable state. She'd covered up her ass with the ocean-like blanket, but her back was still visible. A back I'd run my tongue down just an hour ago. A back made strong from hours in the pool, yet still so female and soft.

Lily was part of my second chance, for sure. And again I told myself to not fuck this up.

"So, anyway," I said, needing to get back on track so I didn't crawl back into bed with her and totally blow off picking up Andy. "The guy who used to work with my father tiling, Frank, went to work at Bribury after my dad died. When I came back from USC, he called and asked if I wanted a job on the facilities crew there. Here," I corrected myself, taking in my surroundings. "He'd worked his way up the past ten years and is head of the maintenance crew."

"That was nice of him, to look out for you."

"Yeah, but I told him no. Told him I was doing okay. I'd moved in with Stick and was…doing some work with him. I was throwing a few bucks my mom's way to help out. And I didn't really want a regular gig like he was offering."

"Because then you couldn't be high all the time." Again, no judgment, just relaying the facts as she guessed them. And, of course, she was right.

"Right. And it was working for a while, and I seemed to think it could go on that way indefinitely." I shook my head at my own idiocy. "Stupid fuck," I said. She didn't argue with me.

"Then I realized my mom was using again. She'd started about a year after my dad died. Party drugs at first with the married scumbag who left her pregnant. I don't think she used when she was pregnant, but I'm not sure. But after that asshole walked away from her, and she'd had Andy, she turned to harder stuff." I had tried to block out those years. Me being fifteen and wanting only to play ball and get laid but having a bawling, squealing, baby half brother at home and a mother who could have been in any kind of shape at any given time. "I kind of checked out then. I wasn't much help to her. I was only looking out for myself."

"You were a kid yourself," she said.

She was right, and I knew that on an intellectual level. But on a gut level? "I was scared and selfish."

"Again, a kid." Her voice was a little firmer now. I nodded, agreeing. I would never totally let myself off the hook for being emotionally AWOL those years, but I was trying to make up for it now.

"Anyway, my mom maintained. A functional junkie, I guess you'd call it. She held down jobs...until she didn't. Andy was always taken care of, but that was also due to Mrs. Jankowski." It was one of the reasons I'd moved into my mom's place instead of taking Andy to the apartment I shared with Stick. Besides that apartment not being a proper environment for a six-year-old, Mrs. Jankowski, being a caring woman who loved Andy and was basically a shut-in, was a godsend.

I waved a hand, not wanting to talk about all this shit anymore. "You know the rest. My mom started using again six months ago. I got clean. I went and saw Frank, asked him if the job was still available. He could have told me to go fuck myself, he would have had every right."

"But he didn't."

I shook my head, my hair getting in my eyes. I pushed it back, off my face. "No. He said if I could pass a drug test, I was hired. Even said there were some tiling projects in the plan for the next couple of years and he thought I'd be a good fit for them."

"He remembered you learned from your dad."

I smiled, as touched now as I was then by Frank's generosity. "Yep. Although I needed to brush up a little. I redid our bathroom at the apartment first. When Frank saw it, he gave me the steam room as the first Bribury project. If I do a good job, he said there are a lot more custom tiling jobs around campus, and the pay will be a lot better than what I'm making now."

"That's great. So, you've go to knock it out of the park with my steam room." She was smiling, and she stretched again, adding to the vision that was forming in my mind for the steam room. And adding to my growing erection.

"Not a problem," I said, leaving my chair and walking the few steps to the bed, and to a naked Lily.

SIXTEEN

Lily

THE NEXT three weeks were a haze of bliss. It wasn't easy with Lucas's hours, Andy, and, of course, classes for me.

And I tried to have a regular life away from Lucas. I desperately didn't want to be one of those girls who dropped everything when she had a new boyfriend. I still went to some parties with Syd and Jane. It kind of did double duty—I wasn't spending every waking moment with Lucas, and I could honestly tell my father when he called that I was hanging closely with Jane. And I did keep an eye on her when we went out, but that was more because I wasn't really interested in anything going on around me.

Oh, it was fun meeting new people, but that was just it… they weren't really new. More like a rehashing of all the other people I'd already met at Bribury. Hell, all the people I'd met my age my whole life.

Syd wasn't of that mold, but God, she was trying to be. Tossing away anything that made her unique. Telling people she was from New York City, never mentioning Queens. She was turning into a Bribury Basic before my eyes, and although she seemed happy about it, it made me a little sad.

So, I'd be at these parties, or in someone's dorm room in the evenings—when I knew Lucas was working—and I'd hold my own in conversations and stuff, but I wasn't really there.

I was in bed with him in my room, at least in my mind. Replaying that first day, and the several other ones we were able to sneak in around my class schedule. Times when he really should have been sleeping. We'd manage to doze a little bit, but not for very long. Yeah, it was definitely the can't-keep-your-hands-off-each-other phase.

One day he picked me up after class and took me back to his place for a glorious few hours before we picked up Andy, and Lucas dropped us both off for Andy's swim lessons.

That was the only time we were "us" in front of Andy. And even that time we just said Lucas had seen me walking in town so he gave me a ride since I was going to the same place Andy was.

The kid was six. He bought it.

I took the requisite amount of shit from Jane about Lucas. She'd make a comment about the place smelling like townie sex when she'd come back from class and knowing that Lucas had been there.

She was exaggerating, of course, but I took to opening the windows a crack while Lucas and I went at it. It was turning out to be a semi-nice fall for the mid-Atlantic, and the air was crisp with just enough of a bite to it to cool off our sweaty bodies after we made love.

And yes, it was more and more making love with Lucas than just casual hookups. Though to be honest, my feelings for Lucas Kade had never been casual.

Now I sat in one of the classrooms at the women's IM building working on my assignment for Montrose's class. And waiting for Lucas's shift to start.

I'd done lessons earlier and Lucas was taking Andy home to feed him and get him to bed before coming back for his shift. He was still using that same car of Stick's, and I made it a point not to ask what Stick expected in return for Lucas using one of his cars.

I tapped the keys on my laptop, trying to put Lucas out of my mind so I could get this damn assignment done. It wasn't due for another week, right before break, but I knew it was going to be a tough one so I wanted to give it as much time as I could.

A three-thousand-word essay that began with the sentence "As I write this today, the person I am is…"

It was supposed to be a self-examination done as a stream-of-consciousness kind of thing. Montrose had said to dig deep, be honest. He had this thought that we would keep them and pull them out in four years when we graduated to see the changes in ourselves.

Simple assignment, even if you just did the surface stuff and didn't challenge yourself as Montrose suggested.

And yet my document was blank, the cursor flashing at me, mocking me.

Let's see, "I am totally a Bribury Basic" would take up about six words. So, 2994 words short.

Maybe I should suggest to Syd and Jane that we swap and write each other's pieces. Not in a cheating kind of way, but I felt I could easily write on both of them so much more easily than trying to find something more about myself to say than what I could pull up in my yearbook bio.

"Hey, you." Lucas's deep voice broke my thoughts. I could have closed my laptop, but my document was still blank other than the intro sentence. "Studying?"

I shrugged. "Trying to write a paper, but it's not coming. Have you been working in the steam room?"

He shook his head, coming to sit at the desk next to me, which he scooted close, the table parts of both of ours touching. "Can't yet. Believe it or not, there are a couple of women swimming in open swim. I need to wait until they're out of the locker room. I've been futzing around the building doing odds and ends until I can get in there."

"Women in the locker room never stopped you before."

He waggled his brows at me. "Totally different sitch. These are women. You are *the* woman. Big difference."

I laughed. He took a peek at my laptop. "'Who I am right now?' Like, in some kind of existential bullshit kind of way? Like where you stand in the universe?"

I shrugged again. "Maybe. I guess. I mean, it's supposed to be a kind of measurement of ourselves. Like, who do we think we are right now. Then we'll look at them when we graduate and see how much we changed."

I saw the moment I lost him. His mind went back to how much he'd changed over the past four years. Where he thought he'd be, and where he was.

I laid a hand on his arm. "Hey, I'm here," I said, though I wasn't sure why, or what I meant exactly.

It seemed to do the trick, though, and he laid his hand on mine, entwining our fingers.

He held my hands like that, over my head, digging into the bed, when he was deep inside me. I think he was remembering that too as he stared at our clasped hands.

"I'm right where I'm supposed to be," he said, looking at me, his brown eyes burning into mine. Into me.

"Me too," I said.

He nodded toward my laptop. "So, write that. Life is good, you're the person you want to be, and you're crazy nuts about your boyfriend."

We'd never said the boyfriend/girlfriend words out loud to each other. Though I knew we were exclusive.

The second time we had sex in my room, he held my hands like he was now and held himself away from me. "You're mine," he'd said, and I knew it wasn't a question.

"Yes, I'm yours," I'd answered, meaning it. Then I'd turned myself, coming on top of him and leaned down, letting my hair fall around us, cocooning us. "And you're mine," I'd said, again with no question, though God, I wasn't as sure of myself as he'd been.

"Yes, I'm yours," he'd said, and flipped me again, driving into me as he pushed my legs up to my chest.

That was all the talk of exclusivity we'd had, but it was all we needed.

"Yes," I said, motioning with my free hand to the laptop, "I can indeed say I'm good and crazy about my *boyfriend*." I emphasized it, so he'd know I was cool with it. Cool with it? Hell, I'd wear his letter jacket and school ring if people still did that kind of shit.

"But then what do I write for the other three thousand words?"

He smiled that killer dirty smile that usually only came out when he was getting me out of my clothes. "What? You can't espouse on my hotness for three thousand words?"

"Seriously? Espouse?"

"I did go to college for three years, you know. Some of it sank in."

"I thought you majored in football?"

He shrugged and sat back in his seat. I disentangled my hand from his and leaned so I could run my fingers through his hair, pushing it out of his face. I never got tired of sinking my fingers into that silky mess. "I could easily *espouse* on how hot you are. For a freakin' novel, let alone three thousand words. But I'm guessing that's not what the prof has in mind."

I sat back in my seat, letting go of him. I checked the time on my phone. "Those ladies have to be out of the locker room by now. You should probably get in there."

We were really careful about spending time together when Lucas was officially on the clock. He couldn't jeopardize this job.

He didn't talk about it much, but I knew there was some legal stuff looming with Andy and his mom and that whole thing.

He looked at his watch. "I've got a couple of minutes. So, tell me who you think you are. Don't worry about getting it down on paper right now."

"I...I...you know me," I said, getting uncomfortable. This was even worse than trying to write it and coming up with nothing.

"I'd like to think I do, yeah. But who do *you* think you are, Lily?"

"I'm…I'm…" I fidgeted in the desk, pulling it a bit a way from him. He readjusted, moving his phone from his pocket to the desk and setting it next to Bribury key ring he carried, seemingly settling in.

I loved to look at him, but I found it easier to speak if I looked away, at the front of the out-of-use classroom. These rooms still had blackboards, not the whiteboards or electronic whiteboards that all the other rooms on campus were equipped with.

In my mind I saw snatches of words, phrases writing themselves on the blackboard. "Alexis's younger sister. Gray's older sister. Grayson and Susan Spaulding's second child." I paused.

"You mentioned your father that night we went to look at the graffiti. Who is he, anyway? I'm assuming politics or some CEO or something."

It was a fair assumption, given the majority of the student population at Bribury came from one of those two worlds. Sometimes both.

"Politics. He's a political consultant. He's run a presidential campaign."

"Did his guy win?"

I didn't want to get too deeply into it. We were now sliding from my story into Jane's, and it wasn't my story to tell. "No. But he's had other big wins."

"So, a kingmaker?" I nodded. "And what's that like to grow up with?"

I tipped my head back, closing my eyes. The blackboard still in my mind, adjectives still writing themselves.

"Exciting. Prestigious. Scary. Nerve-racking. Lonely." Lucas didn't say a word, but I could feel his presence next to me. I always seemed to sense when his body was near mine.

"There were times when I was in awe of my father's genius, of his maneuvering, of his staying a step ahead of…everyone. Most of the time, though, I just wanted to stay out of his way."

"Did your brother and sister do that too?"

I let out a long breath. "No, they're both really…I don't

know, colorful, I guess. Kind of like Jane."

I felt his big hand on my neck, could feel his breath as he whispered in my ear, "Sometimes muted colors are the prettiest ones, the most beautiful. Sometimes bright colors hurt your eyes if you look at them for too long."

Oh God, I felt a tear slide out of my closed eye and down my cheek. Lucas caught it with his thumb, absorbing it.

"What if all I am is truly a Bribury Basic?" I whispered. Another tear slid down. God, so embarrassing. I had no idea where these tears came from. I truly liked the person I was. So what if…what?…there wasn't much substance? I was only eighteen, for Christ's sake. Give a girl a break.

"You are not just a Bribury Basic," Lucas said, squeezing my neck. I heard him get up, the desk screeching across the floor, though his hand stayed on me. I could feel the heat of him as he leaned over my back and kissed the top of my head. "*I* know how much more you are. You just need to figure it out too."

I didn't open my eyes for a long time, and when I did I was alone.

SEVENTEEN

❖

Lucas

I TOOK my dinner break around midnight. I was hungry from all the sanding I'd been doing to prep the steam room, but instead of digging into my packed lunch, I went back to the classroom where Lily had been on the off chance she'd still be there.

Part of me hoped not—she should be back in her room, in bed. But another part of me was hoping that—

There she sat. Well, slumped, actually. Asleep at the desk she'd been sitting in when I'd left her. Her phone was next to her, on mute, but I could see a bunch of missed texts from Jane.

Are you okay? and *Check in, asshole!* I smiled, thinking of Jane's angry fingers typing out of fear.

Lucas here. Lily fell asleep while studying in IM building. I'll walk her home later.

A pause, but not a long one, before, *Thanks.*

"Lily," I said quietly, laying a hand on her back, not wanting to startle her. "Time to go home."

She jerked, her head coming up quickly. So quickly I had to take a step back or she would have head-butted me. "Hey, it's me. You fell asleep."

She nodded, as if she knew that, but she was looking around, taking in the room, her laptop on the desk in front of her, where she'd been resting her head on her arms.

"What time is it?" she asked even as she reached for her phone, which I handed her.

"Midnight." She nodded, and nodded again as she saw my exchange with Jane.

"Are you on your lunch break?" she asked.

"Yep. I'm yours for an hour," I said, stretching my arms wide, as if offering myself to her. Well, shit, I was *always* offering myself to her, whether overtly or not. "More than enough time to walk you to Creyts and back. Maybe even get some goodnight kisses in, too."

"Or…" She stood up, slid her laptop and phone into her backpack, and moved away from the desk. Taking my hand, she led me from the room. I turned the lights off as we left, but instead of turning right to the main door, she took a left, heading back to the locker room. "We could find a better way to spend an hour, and then I can walk home by myself…" She was at the locker room door and she turned, putting her spectacular ass against the door and pushing it open with an awesome flex of her hips. "… after."

Oh, "after" was working all kinds of yes for me.

She locked the door to the locker room behind us and led me through the rows, dropping her backpack at the place I'd come to think of as "Lily's row," even though I'd only been in here one time when she had, that first day I saw her.

Holy shit, it seemed liked yesterday, and a lifetime ago, since I saw Lily Spaulding pull my sputtering baby brother out of the water.

And yet a lifetime didn't seem like enough time to spend with her. Getting to know her better, watching as she got to know herself.

I followed her—shit, I'd follow her anywhere—as she made her way down the row. Peeling off her jacket, she let it fall to the floor as she kept walking. And then came her sweater. With a seemingly effortless flick of her arms, the knit top went by the wayside too, landing on the bench that ran the length of the row in front of the lockers.

Oh, I was liking this.

Her camisole was next, and my Bribury tee joined it on the floor as I followed the soft sway of her hips. Her bra was pink—damn, she had the prettiest bras—and she kept it on, which in a way was even sexier. Her hands moved to her front, and I knew she was unzipping her jeans. She had to stop to slide off her Uggs and then the jeans. I stood where I was, several steps behind her, not taking the opportunity to catch up to her. That would happen soon enough—when she wanted it to. I undid my jeans, untying and kicking off my boots and peeling out of my socks as I kept an eye on her, waiting for her to move again, or for those jeans to shimmy down her long legs.

That was what happened first; the jeans came down, slowly—so fucking slowly!—over her hips, showing the pink of her panties, then the long, shapely thighs. The denim pooled at her feet, and while I was kicking at mine, she gracefully stepped out of her jeans and continued on, to the end of the long row of lockers.

I kept willing her to look over her shoulder, to give me that beguiling smile that she gave me whenever I was deep inside her—or about to be. But she knew she was driving me crazy by not looking back.

She gave the lock on the door to the pool a quick flip—she knew this place well. Her step faltered just a tiny bit as she walked onto the pool deck, but who could blame her. If I was walking out into a pool area in my underwear I'd do a quick look and make sure everybody was indeed long gone.

I knew they were, had locked the door to the locker room myself after the last of the ladies were gone. And I'd waved to Freddy, as he was the last one into the men's locker room. That had been nearly three hours ago, as Lily had worked on her paper and then dozed off.

I stayed slightly behind her as she led the way across the pool deck to the deep end. Just as I was about to reach out and grab her, she took a three-step run and dove into the calm water.

Following her lead, I ran the last few steps and dove in behind her, careful to watch the way she moved under the water so I wouldn't overtake her, or bump into her.

There'd be time for both bumping into her, and, yeah, overtaking her for sure.

She broke surface a few yards in front of me, and though I stayed under water a few more strokes, I followed in her trail.

She swam the length of the pool. I'd follow Lily anywhere, and I was still in pretty good shape from my playing days, but I couldn't keep up with her if she was going to swim some serious laps.

But she stopped at the shallow end, right in the center of the pool, along the wall. I stood up, the water coming to the waistband of my briefs at this end, and just below her bra. The overhead lights were out, but the underwater ones were still on. Windows lined one wall of the pool area, but the women's IM building sat on a hill, so someone would have to be hovering above ground to be able to see into the pool. From outside, though, on campus, the underwater lights sent an eerie glow through the windows. It was kind of cool to see. But I was sure as shit happier to be on the inside—with Lily looking at me like she was right now—than out on campus wondering what the cool glow came from.

The water gently waved from our motions, splashing softly against Lily's tits, just barely seeping over her bra cups, then back down. The pink bra was three shades darker when wet, but I could still see her nipples hardening as I stared at her. Another step closer, and she put her arms up on the gutter ledge on either side of her. It pushed her tits up even higher, as if she was offering them to me.

And yeah, I was going to take what she was offering. And then some.

I reached her, putting a foot between hers and nudging, like a cop. She spread her legs, taking her down just enough that the water level rose to halfway up her bra cups. "Take your panties off," I said, my voice sounding much more sure of myself than I actually felt. This was Lily's show, and maybe she had a vision of how she wanted it go. If she did, she was okay with my command, if the way her breathing hitched was any indication. Her hands and arms left the ledge and pushed down her panties down, her head going under water slightly with the movement, then back up. Her hair was loose—how I loved it—and the wet mass streamed down her back and across her shoulders, a chunk of it falling down her chest, a stark black contrast against the fading tan of her skin and the pink of the bra.

She tried to kick the panties free, but the wet material clung to one of her feet. She started to reach again, but I said, "Leave it." She straightened up, putting her hands back on the ledge. She raised a brow at me.

My move.

I couldn't keep my hands off her…ever. When we were in her bed I'd constantly be touching her, my hands roaming all over her body, wanting to feel every inch of her, wanting to remember her scent, her texture, her taste. Knowing it would have to end sometime. Knowing she would want to experience college as any other freshman, not with a townie boyfriend who worked odd hours and was the caregiver to a six-year-old.

She hadn't yet, and I was going to take full advantage of that fact.

But here, now, in the pool that she loved so much, I held my need to touch her in check, wanting to try something a little different.

"Take my dick in your hand," I said, stepping into her, but not touching. I put my hands on the pool deck above her head, bracketing her. Her right hand left the gutter ledge, reached into my briefs and wrapped around my cock, smooth and silky, just like the water that surrounded us. She stroked me up and down a little, her pressure gentle and firm, and pushing my briefs down.

One afternoon last week in her dorm room I'd taught her exactly how I liked to be jerked off, and she'd four-pointed on the first try. An honor student, for sure.

And then she'd shown me how she liked to be touched…how she did it when it was just her. I thought I'd never seen anything so sexy as Lily touching herself the way she wanted me to touch her.

But this…The hazy underwater lights gave a spooky glow to our skin, the pink panties around her foot a waving blob. Her skin seemed translucent where the lights shone behind her.

She didn't need me to tell her what to do next. Guiding me to her, she lifted a weightless leg and slid me to her entrance. Then she placed her hand back on the ledge, leaning back. Waiting. Daring.

Still without touching her—except for my raging hard cock—I stepped a tiny bit closer and flexed my hips upward, sliding into her.

"Lucas," she said on an exhaled breath. I flexed again.

Her hands left the ledge, then she seemed to catch herself. She looked at me questioningly and I smiled at her, in an almost challenging way.

My tough Lily took the challenge—such as it was—and put her hands back on the ledge, gripping it tightly, as if she didn't trust herself.

We had entered into a game of no-touch chicken, and I was the idiot who started it. She smirked and clenched around me, feeling she had the winning hand. She had the winning body part (hell, parts!), that was for sure. But I didn't make it to Division One football by not being competitive.

I flexed my hips again, driving deeper. She lifted her leg higher against the pool wall, wanting it as deep as she could get it.

So did I.

One of her hands left the wall and I was thinking victory (not that being deep inside Lily Spaulding wasn't victory enough), but no, she instead pulled her bra cup down, over her gorgeous breast. Then the other one, letting the pink material gather below each luscious tit, pushing them up. Right where they'd be so, so easy to bend just a tiny bit and have in my mouth.

"Well played, my little political mastermind," I said.

She barked a laugh. "That's my father, not me," she said as she moved just enough that the water lapped over those pink, pebbled nipples.

"I'm thinking the apple doesn't fall too far from the tree," I said as I withdrew from her, careful not to lose her completely.

"I honestly don't know if that makes me feel good or shitty," she said. She pivoted her hips up a tiny bit, trying to get me deeper. Still the only place where we touched was where I was lodged inside her.

"I can say for sure that you definitely...feel...good." I pushed into her again. "So good. So tight. So wet."

"I'm *all* wet," she said, lifting her hands, letting the pool water sift through her fingers. I thought about all the clever things those fingers had done to me, and I sped up my strokes, causing her to quickly grab the ledge again.

"Lucas," she moaned, leaning her head back against the pool wall.

I worked with tile all day, smooth and fine, common ceramic or precious glass. But right now there wasn't a more beautiful tile than the ages-old stuff that Lily rested her head upon as she took me hard.

"Yes, baby, I'm here," I said, answering her moans. I dug into the pool deck, just above where she rested her head, the cool tile making an imprint in my palms. Her foot slid up the pool wall, her hip flexing out, opening herself as much as she could to me, but still not being the first one to touch each other.

I watched her beautiful face, her eyes closed, her concentration solely on my strokes, matching her muscle tightening with my down stroke, as if she couldn't stand for me to leave her, if only for another hard push into her tight little pussy.

"Jesus, Lily," I said on a groan as I picked up my pace.

And then it all seemed so stupid not to touch her. Sure, it had started as a fun little sex challenge. But to not hold her in my arms, to not feel her shudders as she came? Such a waste. So fucking stupid.

Christ, who knew how long I'd be able to have her in my life? I felt like I was living on borrowed time with her as it was.

My hands came down from the pool deck, skimming her head, tangling in her wet hair. Then I cupped her face, her eyes open now. They didn't shine with the thrill of victory, but were stormy with the same passion that I felt.

I skimmed down to her tits. I knew how much she liked to have those delectable nipples pinched. And I did, much to her delight. But it wasn't enough. I needed to hold those hips, hold her in place as I plunged into her.

Into my Lily.

Her breath caught and I knew she was close. Even after only a few weeks I knew her body's patterns and rhythms.

And I knew I'd never forget them.

My hand moved from her hip to her mound, seeking her clit. The water gave me some resistance, but there would never be enough resistance to keep away from making Lily shatter.

And shatter she did, after only a few targeted circles of my thumb around her pulsating clit.

The sounds she makes when she comes, and the way she shudders around me, it's always enough to make me blow, but I hung on this time. Trying to last, trying to stay hard and inside her as long as I possibly could.

Because, let's face it, being hard and inside Lily Spaulding was my whole fucking world. The magnitude of that thought sent me over the edge, and I came deep inside her.

After abstaining, I couldn't touch her enough, my hands roaming free as the aftershocks rocketed through us both.

My mouth sought hers…so soft, so sweet. And yet strong too, demanding. Wanting my tongue as much as I strove for hers. We danced, parrying and dodging, but in the end, both of us needing the other's mouth so desperately.

My whole body leaned into hers, still joined, still deep inside her. I'd never thought the smell of chlorine could in any way be erotic, but oh how wrong I was.

"You won," I said, holding her close. Never wanting to let her go.

"Oh, Lucas," she said, her voice husky from her moans, "we're all winners here."

I hugged her even tighter, the water not even able to penetrate the nonexistent space between us.

"That we are," I said. Kissing her lightly one last time, I looked into her eyes and repeated, "That we are."

EIGHTEEN

❖

Lucas

"I THINK you'll be fine. There are some loose ends to tie up that will help if CPS decides to become more involved, but"—the lawyer who sat at his desk in front of me flipped through some papers—"we should be able to get the paperwork going right away to make you a legal guardian for…Andy." He had to look at the paperwork to get Andy's name right, which kind of pissed me off. But, I suppose, these guys saw lots of cases like this every day. Just because Andy was my main responsibility didn't mean it was W. Stan Lansing's.

Yeah, that was his name. Stick had found the guy. Said he was the top lawyer in town. I didn't want to ask how Stick would know who was the best lawyer. Though I did clarify that I needed a family law guy, not a criminal lawyer.

Stick had just said, "Fuck you," and given me old W. Stan's business card.

"Thanks," I said to W. Stan.

He nodded, already looking elsewhere on his desk, like for the next guy's file.

And then, as if he remembered what they taught in law school about the lawyer's equivalent of bedside manner, he looked me in the eye and said, "We'll make this happen, Lucas. We'll make sure little Andy is taken care of."

I nodded. That was all I wanted—for Andy to have a shot.

I'd had mine—football. The tear of my shoulder, and then the torment of the taste for painkillers fucked up my shot.

But Andy had a clean slate, and I just wanted to make sure he had the best chance to keep the slate filled with choices.

If that choice was a clean and sober mother to raise him? Excellent.

If it was a big brother who gladly stepped in to pick up the slack because the mother wasn't quite in top form? Well, yeah, that would work too.

But I wanted it on paper. I wanted it legal. I didn't want CPS showing up in two years if my mom had a setback and yanking Andy out of the only home he'd known.

"We'll have the papers drawn up for you to be guardian in the case that Ms. Kade is…" He looked at his notes. I wondered if "junkie" was written in the margins. "…indisposed. For whatever reason." Yep. W. Stan was one smooth, pinstripe-wearing dude.

"Thanks," I said.

"No problem." He stood and reached a meaty hand across his desk for me to shake, which I did gladly. "Janine will talk to you about payments and scheduling and that kind of thing," he said as he sat down, already dismissing me.

"Okay, yeah," I said, dreading talking with Janine, although if she was the receptionist who'd greeted me, she seemed like a very nice older lady.

I made my way out of W. Stan's office and found Janine waiting for me, folder in hand. "Lucas, let's sit over here and talk about things, shall we?"

I'd met some of Stick's less-desirable friends (yes, Stick had friends even less desirable than a reformed Oxy addict and college dropout), but they didn't hold a candle to the gentle but definitely strong-arm tactics of a high-priced law firm and dear, old Janine.

I walked out of their offices feeling great about the chance that Andy would always be looked after by a member of his family in a legal sense.

And totally fucked on how I was going to pay for those assurances.

"You look good, Mom," I said to my mother, honestly meaning it. She looked better than I'd seen her since I'd come home from California.

"I feel good, Lucas," she said. She smiled tentatively, like this well-being could be snatched away at any moment.

She probably thought that was why I was visiting her in the rehab center—to snatch it all away and remind her of the real world awaiting her. The world that had gotten so hard for her that she'd needed to escape. Through chemicals.

No way was I judging...not with my recent past. I totally got it—the escape, by any means necessary.

"You know, one day at a time, and all that," she said, almost embarrassed. Then she sat up a little bit straighter, owning it. "But it's working. It's really working this time."

"That's great, Mom." I believed her. I probably shouldn't have, as I'd been down this road with her before. But there seemed to be something more hopeful in her this time.

Or maybe I just wanted to believe this time was different? Whatever. I took it.

I looked around the place. It was your typical visiting room in a rehab center. The middle-of-the-road kind that's paid for by your job's health insurance. Not one of those beautiful places with views of the ocean or rolling hills to look at as you contemplate your demons. We sat on a comfortable but worn-looking brown leather couch. The place reeked of smoke. Apparently this was one of the places where the inmates could smoke.

"How's Andy? Is he...um...with you?"

"Not with me today, no. They wouldn't have let him in, and I didn't want him out waiting in the hall or anything."

"No. I mean, he's...you're...still in the apartment with him?"

Jesus, had she thought I'd bail on him? Or did she think my being off Oxy was precarious enough that a backslide was on the horizon? It wasn't. I'd been clean six months and was being vigilant about keeping it that way.

"Yeah, Mom. We're doing good, Andy and me. I get him to school and pick him up. We do dinner and I get him to bed. Then Mrs. Jankowski comes over while I work at night."

She nodded like she'd expected nothing less, but her eyes still held some skepticism. "And the job? It's still going okay?"

I nodded. "Yeah, really good. Frank gave me a custom tiling job as a special project. If he likes it, I'll get more of them."

She got a faraway look in her eyes and a sad smile crossed her face. I'd seen pictures, and Linda Kade had been a looker in her day (as much as any son can say his mother was a hottie), but my father's death, Andy's asshole father, several jobs, and the ever-tempting drugs had all taken a toll on her.

She looked ten years older than her forty-three years.

"That's great, Lucas. Your father would be proud of you. Tiling, that is."

She needed to clarify, because there hadn't been a lot of reason lately for my dead father to be proud of me.

But life had given me a second chance, and I was grabbing that motherfucker by both horns.

This could have been me, sitting here like she was. So, so fucking easily. I'd glossed over the details of my Oxy use with Lily that day in her dorm room. The day we'd first slept together. I hadn't told her about all the awful shit that I'd gone through just to get off the stuff. And it was by the sheer grace of God, or the universe, or whatever, that I hadn't already turned to other stuff by the time I realized I needed to get clean so that Andy would have at least one person in his life who wasn't totally fucked.

But it wasn't me in here. It was my mom, and she seemed to be getting the help she needed.

"And no one's been around? Asking questions about why you're there with Andy?"

I debated on how much to tell her, but she'd have to sign whatever papers W. Stan Lansing put together, so it might as well be now. "Well, Andy mentioned to his teacher that you were on a trip and that I was living with him."

"And she reported it to CPS," my mom said, knowing the drill. Sad that she knew so well how the system worked. When Lily didn't even know what CPS stood for.

"Yeah. They came around, saw how we were doing. I gave them Frank's name as a reference for me having a good job. I yanked Mrs. Jankowski over to talk to them about her being with Andy while I worked, when Andy was already in bed." I ran a hand through my hair, thinking back to that nerve-racking visit and waiting to hear back from them. It was the week before I met Lily. It seemed like a million miles away, yet a CPS visit could happen again at any time. "They were cool with the situation. Even said Andy seemed to be dealing well with your...absence."

She grimaced at that. She'd been the one to tell Andy she was going away for a while to "learn to be a better mommy" to him.

Andy hadn't handled it well at all, and it had been slow going at first. But the swimming lessons helped—it kept him busy a couple of the days after school, and then exhausted at night. I took him to the park to play catch and stuff on the other days. He still missed our mother and would get upset at times, but he seemed to be adjusting okay. I tried to keep an eye on it as best as I could—talking with his teacher, and, of course, deep, deep discussions with his swimming instructor.

"The thing is, Lucas," my mom was saying now, pulling me away from my thoughts about just what other things Andy's swim instructor was doing on a deep level. "I'd like to stay here a bit longer. My month is up in a few days." Which I knew—that was one of the reasons why I was here today, to discuss plans for when she came home. Would she still want me to stay there? Could I help her in her recovery more by being there, or giving her and Andy more space?

"But I'd really like to stay another thirty days," she said. She quickly went on when I didn't say anything. "My doctors think it's a good idea too. But if you can't stay with Andy—"

I held up a hand. "I can stay with Andy as long as you need. That's not a problem. I can move back permanently even when you're back home if that will help you out."

"Oh, no, I'd never ask you to do that, Lucas. You're a man now, and you have your own life to live."

Yeah, and I'd done such a stellar job of that so far. "Well, not forever, but until Andy's older."

"You're going to want to settle down yourself soon, Lucas. You're not going to want to be living with your mother and little brother."

Lily had three and a half more years at Bribury before we even thought about what we'd do after she graduated. Whether we'd stay here in Schoolport, or go elsewhere. Although that didn't mean that we couldn't live together while she finished Bribury. Maybe her junior year we'd—

My thoughts screeched to a halt as I realized how completely— and how easily—I'd woven Lily into my future.

And just how right it felt.

And who knows, while Lily was getting her degree, maybe I could look into finishing up mine. I'd done okay at USC—for a jock—and probably only needed a year and a half to complete a degree. I was pretty sure there was even a break on tuition for Bribury employees, for continuing education purposes. No doubt an effort on the administration's part to reach out to the community that served the college's needs. It made them look good.

"I'm going to be around and available for a few years yet," I said to my mom, not willing to talk to her about Lily right now. This visit wasn't about how happy I was with Lily, it was about my mom's fight. "And I think it's great you want to stay another thirty days."

She leaned across the table and put her hand on top of mine. Hers was cold and had just the slightest tremble to it as she grasped mine.

"Thank you, Lucas. I really think I'm going to make it this

time. It feels different."

Which, actually, was something my mother had never said before, and so I believed her. "Whatever you need, Mom." And then reality crashed in. "Will your work insurance pay for the extra thirty days?"

Her hand clenched a tiny bit, and she pulled it away. "They'll pay for fifteen, forty-five total days. And, of course, I don't get paid while I'm in here. But I am guaranteed my job when I get out. I have some money put aside, not much, and it was supposed to go for the rent on the apartment while I was here."

I was doing the math in my head. I made better money on the third shift at Bribury than I would have on first, but I was just starting out and the pay wasn't great. It was enough to help, but not enough for rent, food, and everything else.

My mom's eyes flickered away from me, taking in the room around her, as if she wanted to get her last looks in because it would soon be taken away from her. Her hands folded onto themselves, and she began picking at her nails.

"We'll be fine. I've got it covered with my job. Use the money for this place."

She looked at me with hope in her eyes, a look I hadn't seen in a very long time. I swallowed down a lump in my throat. I would make damn sure she was able to live out this newfound hope for her future.

She was my mother and I loved her. When my father had been alive, she'd been a great mom, and we'd been a very close family unit. Even with all the shit that happened after my dad died, she still did the best she could, and I always knew that she loved me, and wanted to do right by me. It was that sometimes she just…couldn't.

I would find a way to take care of the bills so she could be in here as long as she needed to be.

Speaking of huge bills I had no way of paying…

"I spoke with a lawyer yesterday about putting something in place to make me a legal guardian of Andy for when you're in here, or if…" I didn't want to go there, didn't want to say, "If this ever happens again."

But she knew. With a sad smile, she said, "That was a good idea. It's best to have something in place, just to keep CPS off your back a bit."

"Yeah. So, they're going to have something ready in a week or so." (Or whenever I could pay Janine the fee for it.) "And I'll bring it here for you to look over and sign."

She nodded. "Make sure that it's you only, Lucas, that's listed."

"Who else would I put on it?" Stick helped out with Andy more than he had to, and had actually been pretty cool with me having to move out of our apartment and back in with Andy, but he wasn't legal guardian material by any stretch. I couldn't think of anyone else.

"I mean, not that I think that asshole would care. But I do not want Andy's father showing up now and demanding custody or anything because he heard I was in here."

A cold chill ran down my spine as I thought about the man who gave my mom her first taste of drugs…cocaine at a party. "You don't seriously think that's a possibility, do you?"

The guy had been married, and had dropped her when she was pregnant with Andy. I never knew what happened to him; he lived in Chesney, not Schoolport. But now I wondered if my mom had kept tabs on him. She had given Andy the guy's last name, I think hoping that he'd step up and acknowledge Andy. Never happened.

"No, I don't think it's likely. But if he knew I was in here…"

"He'd all of a sudden care about the well-being of his son, after not giving a flying fuck for six years?" She flinched, but I wasn't sure if it was because of my language or the raised voice. "Sorry," I said softly, apologizing for both.

"I shouldn't have even brought it up. It's so unlikely. But it just makes me feel even better that you went to see a lawyer, Lucas. I should have thought about it myself before I came in here." She let out a strangled chuckle. "But I wasn't in any shape to think about something like that."

"I'll call the lawyer and tell him about Andy's father. Make sure that we have that base covered."

She was nodding. "Yes. Yes. Thank you so much, Lucas. It's so much easier to spend the time in here on things I need to work on when I don't have to worry about Andy."

As a son who had given his mother much to worry about when she hadn't needed it, it felt good to say, "Just take care of yourself, Mom. I've got the rest of it."

Tears streamed down her worn face, but they were tears of relief.

I'd find a way, I silently told myself, as I once again held my mother's hand.

NINETEEN

Lily

"I HAVE to go," I said to my mother on the phone as I got a text from Lucas saying he was outside the dorm. "I've got a date," I said before I thought better of it. But I'd been thinking about it all day, so it just kind of popped out.

"Oh, who's the boy?" she asked with keen, lawyer-like interest, which was exactly why I shouldn't have said anything.

Lucas was my everything, but I wasn't shrewd Grayson Spaulding's daughter for nothing. "Just a first date. We'll see how it goes."

It was not technically a lie. This was our first actual date. True, we'd been sleeping together for weeks, but tonight was our first "pick you up, dinner and a movie, drop you off (okay, spend most of the night making sweet, sweet love)" date.

"Keep me posted on him," she said.

"I will if it turns into anything." Which I knew I'd have to do soon, probably over the upcoming Thanksgiving break. Especially because I was considering staying here instead of taking the train to DC so I could be with Lucas for four whole uninterrupted days. My body shivered with yearning just thinking about it.

"Oh, your father wants to talk to you."

"Mom, I really have to—"

"Here he is. Bye, sweetie, love you."

"Love you too, Mom," I said. I grabbed my jacket and made my way out of my room as I waited for my father's voice.

"Lily, how are you?"

"I'm good, Dad, how are you doing?"

"Fine, fine. Listen, I wanted to talk to you about Jane."

I walked past the elevator, deciding to take the far stairwell, where it was less likely that anyone would hear me speaking with my father. "She's doing great. I think she's four-pointing all her classes."

"That's good." He didn't ask how my grades were doing, which I guess was just as well. I was hanging on, but I had to work my ass off to do it. Good thing Lucas worked nights or I wouldn't have gotten all the studying in I had over the past several weeks. And I still hadn't made any headway on Montrose's "the person I am today" paper.

"I appreciate whatever help you may have been to her."

I snorted. "Dad, I am no help whatsoever to Jane when it comes to getting good grades. She's probably borderline genius."

"Really?" he said, sounding genuinely surprised. As far as I knew, my father had never actually met Jane. Well, maybe when she'd been a baby and there was all the subterfuge, but certainly not in the past sixteen years. And yet I was willing to bet he knew her high school GPA. He probably knew mine too, but only to make sure I wasn't letting down the family name like Alexis had in school. (I hadn't. I did what was expected.)

"Well, that's good to hear. And she's staying out of trouble? Nothing embarrassing is going to show up online, is it?"

I thought about that night Stick pulled her out of the club in Chesney. Nothing had surfaced after that night—and I'd checked. Frequently. I did *not* want to get the call that my father had seen something about Jane before I had.

"Nope. Clean as a whistle. Just good old-fashioned college freshman fun."

"Hmmm. I was a college freshman once too, Lily," he said with a bit of humor in his voice.

He could be controlling and demanding, and lots of other negative "ing"s, but he also taught me to ride a bike and how to swim. And I loved him, even if I felt I could never truly please him.

But I was beginning to realize that was more on him than me.

"We're being good, Dad," I said.

"And you've become close? You and Jane? Would you say you're friends as well as roommates?"

I slowed on the stairs. "Yes, I'd say Jane is my best friend here. We're both close with our suitemate Sydney, but Jane and I are… tighter."

I knew Jane and Syd were spending more nights together when I was with Lucas, but that wasn't too often with him working third shifts. He had Friday and Saturday nights off every week, working Sundays through Thursday nights, but he didn't like imposing on Mrs. Jankowski his nights off, so he stayed home with Andy.

Sometimes I'd come over, but we were still careful to not be too couple-y around Andy. And we never had sex when Andy was in the apartment.

But there was some major fully clothed humping that went on.

"Just how much influence do you have on Jane?" my father asked, pulling me back from my fond remembrances of being beneath Lucas on his couch.

"Not much. Jane's kind of her own person."

"Hmmm. Well then, she has more backbone than either of her parents."

"I would guess that's probably true." I couldn't see Jane messing around once she was married, or becoming involved with a married man either.

But seducing her Intro to Creative Writing prof? Um, hell yeah.

"Well, listen, a word or two from you about her standing in

her sister's wedding would—"

"Whoa, Dad, let me stop you right there. I don't have much sway over Jane. There is no way she is going to stand in that wedding. Her heels are dug in on that, and once Jane digs in her heels…"

"Still, Lily, it wouldn't hurt for you to mention it."

This. This was why I was at Bribury and not Maryland. This was why I was Jane Winters' roommate.

It wasn't all just keeping tabs on Jane and trying to make sure no naked pictures of her ended up on myporn.com.

It was for moments like this when I would be asked to leverage my friendship with Jane for whatever reason my father—and hers—found imperative.

"Dad, no," I said, the words together like that feeling strange on my tongue. I didn't often combine them to form a sentence.

"Just think about it. It's one day out of her life, and it would be important."

I couldn't figure out why, and neither could Jane, but I wasn't going to ask my father. If I did, and he told me, I'd have to share that with Jane, and then she'd know I'd been talking about her with my father.

Even though she guessed I did.

"Dad, first of all, it wouldn't do any good. And second, I think she would dig in even further if I asked her to think about it." He started to say something, but I spoke over him (which was also new). "Plus then I'd lose all credibility with her." Which was important to me, but I knew that would be the kicker for my father.

"Right. Right. Okay, if you don't think you could sway her, best to just not even bring it up." Always the tactician, my father.

"Good, I won't." I again started down the last flight of stairs, feeling bad that Lucas had been waiting outside for me, even though I'd texted him that I'd be right down.

"Okay, I've got to go," I said.

"Did I hear your mother ask you about a boy? Are you seeing

someone, Lily?"

"Yes. Well, I have a date tonight."

"Would I know this boy's parents?"

You might think that was a stupid question, but the odds were my father *did* know the parents of half the boys at Bribury.

He just didn't know Lucas wasn't a Bribury boy.

"I doubt it. He's—oh, he's waiting for me downstairs," I said, like I'd just gotten the text from Lucas. "I really have to go, Dad."

"Okay, Lily. Be good."

"I will. Bye," I said, and ended the call as I walked through the doors to see Lucas leaning against the pillar.

His smile as I walked toward him made me forget Jane, my father, and pretty much anything other than spending a date night with Lucas Kade.

TWENTY

Lily

"SO, WHAT'D you think of the movie?" I said as we waited for our burgers.

There was no way I should feel nervous with Lucas—he'd seen me first thing in the morning, soaking wet, and had inspected every inch of my body. But sitting in a booth at a burger joint on the part two of our movie and dinner date? It just felt kind of weird.

"Huh? Oh. Um, yeah, it was okay, I guess. Bordered on chick flick, but enough blood and guts to keep it interesting."

"Now see, I was thinking less blood and guts and a little more of the couple and it would have been better."

He shrugged and smiled a little lopsided grin. "Yeah, well."

I reached across the booth table and touched his hand. It had been hard to tell during the movie, but now it seemed obvious to me that something was on his mind.

"Andy okay?" I asked.

"Mmm-hmm," he said, and took his hand from mine to take a drink of his Coke. I leaned back on my side of the booth, trying not to be hurt that he took his hand away. Trying not to read anything into it.

"Your mom? She's doing all right in rehab?"

He nodded. "Yeah. Actually, she's doing really well. It seems to be really helping her…"

There was a "this time" at the end of that sentence, but he didn't say it. "That's great," I said.

He nodded again, not looking at me, eating some of his fries. Finally he sighed heavily and said, "That night in the pool? A couple of weeks ago?"

"Uh…yeah?" Like I was going to forget that night.

"We didn't use anything. I didn't use a condom."

That was what was bothering him? "It's okay, I'm on the pill."

"You are?"

I nodded, ate a couple of my fries. They were extra greasy, just how I liked them.

"Recently?"

"No. I went on it last year."

He was taking this in, and I realized that I probably could have saved him some worrying since that night in the pool. But then, he hadn't told me he'd been worried, had he?

"I'm sorry I didn't say anything after that night in the pool. Honestly, it didn't occur to me." I went to touch him again, but he'd moved both hands to his sides, beneath the table. "I'm sorry you've been worrying about it all this time."

He looked a little embarrassed. "I wasn't. Worrying about it since then. I thought about it after you left, but then…with everything else that's going on, I didn't think about it again until just now for some reason. I'm glad you're protected, that we're covered."

"What's the 'everything else that's going on'?"

He shrugged, looking out the window of the restaurant to the streets of Schoolport. "Nothing for you to worry about. It'll work itself out."

"Hey," I said, gently but with some firmness in my voice. I waited until he looked away from the window and met my eyes. "What's going on? Talk to me."

He looked at me, his glance gliding over my face. Almost like he was trying to memorize me, and I had a moment of panic that he was going to end it.

Finally he sighed heavily and said, "My mom's doing great, like I said. She's going to stay in rehab another month. I'm having legal documents drawn up that make me a legal guardian for Andy if she's not able to…parent."

"Oh…wow…okay, that is a lot going on. And here I am just worried about that stupid 'who am I' paper."

He reached across the table, taking my hand in his. "That's all you *should* be worried about, Lily. Papers and studying and where the next party's at. You don't need to hear about guardianships and rehab and all the other shit going on with me."

I entwined my fingers with his, both our wrists resting on the table. "I'm not dealing with it, you are. I just want to be a supportive girlfriend and allow you to, I don't know, vent or whatever, when you need to. You don't need to…shield me from your life, Lucas. I care about what's going on in your world, even if I can't help, or even understand it sometimes."

He smiled and the tension eased from my chest. Then his smile turned to that dirty grin and I reached for my purse and jacket.

I held him in my arms while he was still inside me, staring down at me, his hair falling along the sides of his face.

Jane had volunteered to stay in Syd's room, in Megan's deserted bed, so Lucas and I could have the room for the whole night, it being such a rare thing.

And we'd taken advantage of it, tearing our clothes off and going at it as soon as we'd entered the room.

But then we'd taken our time, touching and smiling and gazing at each other before Lucas had taken me so tenderly and sweetly, that it brought tears to my eyes.

"Hey," he whispered, "why the tears?" His thumb wiped away the moisture from my cheeks.

"That was just…wonderful. I'm just happy, that's all."

He exhaled what sounded like relief. "Oh, okay. Happy tears

I can deal with. Happy tears are good."

I wrapped my arms tighter around him and he moved off me, to his side, rolling me with him. I hitched a leg up to his hip so he stayed inside me.

"Happy tears are very, very good," I agreed, kissing him.

We lay like that for a while. At some point he slid out of me and I readjusted myself to put my head on his chest, his arm firmly around me, his other hand resting on my hip.

We'd both set our phone alarms for six—so there was no chance we could sleep through just one—when Lucas would have to get up to be home for Andy, and to relieve Mrs. Jankowski.

I could feel myself starting to doze into a sweet oblivion when Lucas said, "Are you still awake," in a soft whisper.

"Yes."

"Turn on the lamp for a sec."

I reached over and turned on the bedside lamp. "What? Do you need to get up?" I started to slide out of the small bed, but he stopped me with a hand on my waist, pulling him back to him.

"No, I don't need to leave. I wish I never had to leave."

I smiled, burrowing into him, kissing his neck, loving the feel of his five o'clock shadow. "I don't want you to."

"But I need to tell you something."

I looked up into his eyes. "Yes?" I cautiously said.

He took my face in his hands. "I love you, Lily Spaulding. I have no idea what my future holds. Hell, I'm not even sure what the next month holds. But I am deeply...*deeply*...in love with you."

"Lucas," I whispered, and softly kissed him. "I love you too."

"You do? Because you don't have to say it just because—"

"Shhhh," I said, my finger on his mouth, which I replaced with my lips for another kiss. "I mean it. I love you."

His eyes welled up with unshed tears. "Jesus, Lily, you're the best second chance anyone ever got. I can't believe you love me too."

"Lucas," I said, "I've loved you from the moment I saw you."

He smiled, thinking I was kidding. He pulled me to him and again I rested my head on his chest, knowing I wasn't kidding in the least.

TWENTY-ONE

Lucas

I'D JUST gotten Andy to bed, after reading him *Where the Wild Things Are* for the forty billionth time, when there was a knock at the door. Used to be, a knock at the door at nine on a Saturday night was a signal that the night was just getting started. But these days, a knock as I was putting Andy down, and ready to hit the hay early myself, was very unusual.

As I made my way down the hall from Andy's room to the door, I wondered if Lily was surprising me. When I left her dorm room this morning, we had decided I'd just stay in with Andy tonight and she'd work on that paper she was struggling with.

I smiled, happy that she had decided to ditch that idea and come pay me a visit. Though I worried about how she got to this side of town on her own.

But it wasn't Lily at the door. It was Stick.

"See, I knocked this time. I hope it didn't wake the kid."

"It didn't. He just went out. Why didn't you just call or text?" I moved away from the door, letting Stick in.

He went right to the fridge and grabbed himself a beer. He offered one to me, but I shook my head no. Twisting the cap off, then taking a long swig, he moved into the living room and sat in the chair. I followed and sat down on the couch.

"Because I needed to talk, and I didn't want to do it on the phone." He leveled his gaze at me and I knew what was coming.

"No. I said I was done with it, and I meant it."

He held up a hand. "Hear me out."

"I don't need to hear about it. No."

"It's tonight. Right now. One car. I've been waiting months for the right time for this car and this is it. You can get Mrs. Jankowski to come over here for two hours. That's all it will take. Two hours of your time. Ten thousand dollars."

"Ten thousand? Are you serious?"

He nodded, took another swig of his beer. Now I wished I'd said yes to one.

Stick dealt in stolen cars. A broker of sorts. He had "clients" that contacted him with specific cars that were desired by their "buyers," and Stick delivered. And I mean *specific* cars. Right down to the color of the interior.

Stick knew about every luxury sedan and expensive sports car that was purchased in a hundred-mile radius, which included several very wealthy enclaves.

This wasn't just smash-and-grab jobs done in the streets of Schoolport.

No. Stick, at the young age of twenty-one, had put together an informational network that would rival that of the CIA.

He had the valets, of course. But what thief worth his salt didn't?

The valets at the swanky places in town, and neighboring towns, would call Stick when a desired car was dropped with them. Stick would swing by, or at one time I would, and get all the information available from spending ten minutes inside the car.

Think about how much you could learn about somebody from spending ten minutes in their car.

Name and address are easy, from the insurance forms in the glove box. GPS could call up the places they'd programmed in. Places they might return to in their car. You could easily tell whether they had kids, if they ate takeout a lot. All sorts of information.

Stick collected all this information and stored it away. He also had this magic gizmo that he'd had some brainiac tech guy make for him. It looked like a regular garage door opener remote, but if you pressed it at the same time you pressed a real garage door remote, it somehow copied the signal code, creating a duplicate remote. It worked the same with gate opener remotes for the posh gated communities.

And, of course, with the valet system you had access to the keys. If he had time while the car owners were dining, Stick would drive a couple of towns away (not going back to the same town without a month or two in between) and have a duplicate car key made. If there wasn't enough time, he just made an impression on the spot and had the key made later.

Stick had seven or eight valets throughout the area in his pocket.

But his network didn't stop there. Hairdressers. Massage therapists. Postal clerks. All people who knew when folks were going on vacations or would be out of town for a while.

Stick wasn't stupid enough to steal someone's car the night after they'd been somewhere with valet service—that would have caught up with him within a month.

Stick was smarter than that. And patient. He kept tabs on a car, as if he was stalking an ex-girlfriend or something.

When, say, an "order" for a Cadillac Escalade in crystal red with shale leather interior came up, Stick only had to make a couple of phone calls to find out that the owner of that car would be going to Jamaica in three weeks. By then Stick would have had that car's address, garage code, and a set of keys for months, just waiting.

Because of being patient, Stick didn't get caught. And none of the car owners thought it important to mention that they'd eaten at a restaurant with valet service three months earlier when reporting their stolen car to the police.

There were snags, of course. Home security cameras were, I

knew, a big detriment to Stick's…access to the cars. But he must have his ways around that, because he seemed to be doing all right for himself.

And he kept his network well taken care of for their information.

I had stolen cars twice for Stick when I'd needed the money for Oxy. Mostly I'd been the guy who showed up when the valets called. My speed would come in handy if I needed to run from a car if people who shouldn't be walking by walked by. Though that had never happened.

"Why so much?" I asked. I wasn't seriously considering it—that life was behind me—but that amount was double what it would normally pay.

"A few reasons. One, I've been waiting for this car for a while. Two, it's short notice and has to happen tonight, so the pay is extra. Three—"

I held a hand up to stop him. "Never mind. I don't really need to know. I'm not interested."

"Come on. I know you need the money. And I need someone I can rely on for this one. Two hours out of your life and your problems disappear."

It was tempting to make all my problems disappear. But that was why the Oxy had been so delicious, so all-consuming—it made everything disappear.

Then you sober up, and you still can't play football anymore.

But I *did* sober up. It hadn't been easy, but I'd done it. And I did face my problems. And yeah, I had one right now with needing money, but I'd find a way. A legitimate way.

Because life was going too well right now to rock the boat. Andy was adjusting. The steam room job was going well and would probably lead to more. My mom was rehabilitating. And Lily? Lily Spaulding was in love with me.

I could not jeopardize any of it, but I especially couldn't lose Lily.

She was what made the rest of it all bearable.

"Pass," I said firmly. I rose from the couch as if calling this meeting to an end.

Stick stayed seated, a man with his own agenda.

"Would it make a difference if I told you the car belonged to George Bell?"

George Bell. Andy's father. That shitbag asshole who dumped my pregnant mother after he'd gotten her hooked on drugs. A guy who never even acknowledged Andy, let alone paid one dime of child support.

"Keep talking," I said as I sat back down on the couch.

TWENTY-TWO

Lucas

I GOT caught. Of course I got caught. I'd seen enough movies where the "last big heist before we retire" was always the one where they got pinched.

Usually in those movies there's a shootout and our hero bites it.

No shootout here. But then again, I'm no hero.

It wasn't Stick's info—that had been solid. And the clicker to the gated community and the garage door both worked with no issues.

But apparently young Eliza Bell—the thirteen-year-old half sister to my half brother—came down with the mumps, and so the family's overnight visit to Grandma's had been postponed at the last minute.

Certainly something Mrs. Bell's hairdresser would not have known about two days ago when she gave Mrs. Bell highlights.

And had then given Stick a call.

I made it out of the driveway, but not out of the gated community before two patrol cars cornered me.

George Bell was running down the cul-de-sac, his bathrobe flying around his pajamas, his cell phone in his hand.

It was almost worth it to see his shocked face when he saw me getting out of his beloved Jaguar XK (Italian racing red with the jet leather interior) with my hands in the air.

Well, no, it was nowhere near worth it. But it did give me a sick thrill to see him stop, and then cautiously walk toward me. He looked around wildly, like maybe he was thinking my mother would pop out of nowhere.

"Hello, George," I said.

I'd been fifteen when he'd dumped my mother and gone back to the family that he'd never really left.

"Mr. Bell, do you know this man?" one of the cops asked him.

I arched a brow at him, daring him to explain how he knew me.

That cold look that he'd give my mother when she'd harp on him about staying over or being with her instead of his wife spread across his rat bastard face.

"I've never seen him before. Obviously I—my car—was his target. It was parked in the garage, not on the street. That must be how he knows my name."

I snorted and saw the officers exchange questioning looks.

"Just to be clear, sir," one of them said to George, "you did not give this man permission to drive your vehicle?"

"I did not," George said, and I felt myself being slammed against the side of the patrol car and being asked to assume the position, which I did.

I thought about running for it. I knew I could outrun any Schoolport cop. Shit, I was a Division One wide receiver, able to outrun any defensive secondary in the nation.

But that was in another life.

In this life my hands were being placed behind my back and those zip-tie things were being placed on me.

My first thought was Stick would have seen the police cars rushing past him where he sat three blocks away, waiting for me to meet up with him so we could take the Jag to his buyer, wherever that was.

Stick would wait until he saw me in the cop car and then he'd make sure to get to Andy. He'd either get Mrs. Jankowski to stay with Andy all night, or he would himself. Then he'd bail me out—

Fuck. It was Saturday night. I wouldn't be arraigned and able to make bail until Monday.

Stick would make sure Andy would get to school on Monday and then come bail me out. Assuming I was granted bail, which wasn't a given.

But then what? Add the cost of a defense to my tab with W. Stan Lansing? Maybe plea down to something with minimal jail time?

In the meantime, I would surely lose my job at Bribury, and either my mother would need to leave rehab, or Andy would be scooped up by CPS, placed in foster care.

Shit, that could happen even *if* my mom left rehab early.

And there was no way in hell I'd be granted a legal guardianship with no job and charges pending or a conviction.

Total clusterfuck, and I had only myself to blame.

And then I thought of losing Lily, and the pain doubled.

TWENTY-THREE

Lily

A POUNDING on my dorm room door woke me up at midnight. I looked over and saw Jane's bed was empty. She must have lost her key. I got out of bed and walked to the door, but it wasn't Jane.

"Are you Lily Spaulding?" a girl who seemed vaguely familiar asked me. I was pretty sure she lived in Creyts, but I knew she didn't live on this floor.

"Yes."

"Oh, thank God. You're like the fourth room I've tried. There's a guy out front says he needs to talk to you. He didn't know your room number, just that he thought you lived on the third floor, but said it was important."

So, not Lucas. Lucas absolutely knew my room number, having spent last night here with me, as well as all those lovely stolen hours when I didn't have class and Andy was in school. Plus he would have texted me that he was downstairs.

"Says his name is Stick. Listen, if you don't want to—"

"No, I want to see him. Thanks for finding me."

She shrugged. "Guy gave me twenty bucks. Easy twenty bucks."

"Thanks again," I said as I left her to throw on a hoodie, yoga pants, and some shoes. I grabbed my phone and keys and quickly made my way down the stairs, texting Lucas as I did.

Did you send Stick over here?

No answer, but he could be asleep and have his phone on vibrate.

I had visions of Stick standing out front holding up a drunken Jane that he'd pulled out of yet another club.

Shit. The one Saturday night when I stayed home to study. That was what I got for studying on a Saturday night when I should have been out partying with Jane and Syd.

But he was alone, no Jane in sight. He was leaning on the pillar as Lucas always did, but straightened, and walked toward me when he saw me.

"What's going on?" The look on his face caused a chill to run down my spine. "What's happened?"

"Let's go up to your room," he said, looking around, motioning to the students that were returning to the dorm. He wanted privacy to tell me what he needed to say.

"Is he okay? Is he hurt?"

Stick shook his head, taking my arm and leading us back inside, using my ID to swipe us in. "He's fine. I mean, he's not hurt or anything. Physically he's fine."

We got to the elevator, but a couple of girls got in with us so we didn't say anything.

During the ride up and the walk down the hallway, I had this crazy thought that maybe Lucas had sent Stick to break up with me. He had been acting weird last night, pulling away from me at the restaurant.

But then he'd told me he loved me.

And sending Stick to dump me would be the most monumental dick move ever. Lucas had promised—no more dick moves.

When we got to my room, my hands were shaking and I turned on Stick as soon as the door had closed. "What? What is it?"

"Lucas is in jail, and I need you to come and stay with Andy while I get it worked out."

I walked to the desk and sat in the chair. Placing my shaking hands on my knees, I took a deep breath. "Oxy? Was it Oxy somehow?"

Stick looked at me like I was crazy. "No. No way. He's totally clean."

"Well, he's not exactly 'clean' if he's in jail, is he?" I almost didn't recognize my own voice.

"No. He was busted for stealing a car." He ducked his head.

"Yeah, you better duck your head, asshole," Jane said from the doorway. I hadn't even noticed her coming in. "So Lily's guy is in the pokey. Why do I think this all circles back to you?" Jane said to Stick as she shut the door and came into the room. She was dressed in casual jeans, not club wear. I didn't know where she'd been, but she wasn't at all tipsy. She came over to me and placed a hand on my shoulder. "You okay, Lil?"

I nodded. "How often…when does…"

Stick stepped toward us. "This is the first job he's done for me in forever. He's really given it all up. He told me he told you the whole story. I just want you to know he wasn't lying to you. This was a one-time thing and it all just came together tonight."

I gave a skeptical look while Jane snorted.

"No. Seriously. He was doing me a solid. And you know he needed the money for all the legal stuff they're trying to do for Andy, and to pay for his mom's extended rehab stay."

No, I hadn't known that part. Not about him hurting for money. Not that I could have done anything to help on that front. I think Grayson and Susan might have had a few choice words if I came to them asking for money for my boyfriend's mother's rehab costs.

But I would have done it if it would've kept Lucas from resorting to going back to that life.

"It was a favor to me. All the cards fell into place for tonight and I needed his help. He did it for me."

"And the money," Jane added.

"Yeah, that too."

"So, okay, you've told her. Time to take your Grand Theft Auto ass back to your side of town and leave us Bribury Basics the hell alone. We may all be lemmings, but we sure as shit aren't car thieves."

"Wait," I said. "What did you mean you need my help with Andy?"

He looked around the room, and I knew he was thinking of a way to spin whatever it was he planned to say. "I think I can have it all taken care of by Monday so that nothing shows up on his record. But I need you to stay with Andy tomorrow and into Monday while I make that happen. Mrs. Jankowski's not up to being with Andy all day when he's awake. And Andy knows and likes you. It won't freak him out to have you staying with him."

"What are you going to be doing?" I had visions of Stick, like, I don't know, killing a witness or something on Lucas's behalf. Probably a bit too harsh, but what did I know?

"I'm…I'm going to turn myself in. Trade myself for Lucas."

"Can you even do that?" Jane asked.

Stick shrugged. "The DA can make that call. And let's just say he's been jonesing for me for a long time."

"If he's aware of you, why aren't you in jail too?"

"He's never caught me in the act, or with stolen goods."

"Yeah, because you get others to do it," Jane said.

"I take as many risks as anyone who…works for me. More." He shook his head, sighed. "Listen, we don't need to get into it all." He looked at me. "Are you willing to stay with Andy while I make a deal with the DA? It could take a few days, and Lucas might not be released until it's all hashed out."

"So, you just take his place? Like it was you who stole the car? Who's going to buy that?"

"No, it's not like that. I have…information…names that the DA has been after for a long time. I give him some…locations where he might find some more cars, take the rap for the attempt to steal the Jag. Do some time, but not too long. And Lucas is home with Andy, no smears on his record to throw CPS on his trail."

"So, you're a bigger fish in all this than Lucas," Jane said, like she needed clarification.

I honestly didn't give a shit. I just wanted to get my stuff and get to Lucas's apartment. I couldn't stand the thought of him in jail, and I wanted to be closer to him. I also wanted to be there for Andy.

"Just let me pack a few things," I said. I started to rise, but Jane's firm hand pushed me back into the chair.

"Hang on, let's just think about this for a second."

"What's to think about?" Stick said to Jane.

"You may not be the only person in this room who can make a deal."

Stick looked from Jane to me, then back to Jane. "Do you know who Lily's father is?" Jane asked.

A tiny glimmer of hope flickered within me. And then it was quickly extinguished when I thought of what I would have to do.

"Who's your father?" Stick asked me suspiciously.

"Someone who that DA of yours would probably love to do a favor for. Isn't that right, Lily?"

I nodded, my body going numb.

"Okay, fine. Wait until I turn myself in, and then make the pity call to Daddy. I'm not too proud to take some help from a bigwig."

Jane shook her head as she stepped from behind me, and handed me my phone. "That won't work. Grayson Spaulding might stick his neck out and ask a small favor for his daughter of getting a petty *first-time* offender…?" She raised a brow at Stick, wanting confirmation that Lucas was indeed a first-time offender. Stick nodded. "But there's no way he's going to go so far out on a limb as to get somebody the DA is 'interested in' off. He's too smart to owe that big of a favor. It's better that it's Lucas."

My phone was slippery in my sweaty hands. I ran my thumb along the long edge, up and down. Knowing I would do anything for Lucas and heartbroken—and pissed—that it had come to this.

But it wasn't just for Lucas. It was for Andy too.

"You, asshole," Jane said, patting Stick on his shoulder as she passed him, "are our Plan B. But let's see if we can't keep the both of you out of prison, shall we?" She went to my closet and pulled out a duffle bag.

"Make the call, Lily, while I pack your bag."

TWENTY-FOUR

Lily

I CALLED up my home landline from my contacts and connected. "Do you want to be alone?" Stick asked. I shook my head. I wanted some reinforcements in case my courage failed me. I would be brave in front of Jane.

She seemed to sense it, because she slowly walked around the room, picking up a couple of things and putting them in the bag.

"Lily?" my father answered. "It's after midnight. What the hell—"

"Lily, honey, are you all right?" my mother said from the extension. That was why I'd called the landline; they each had a phone on their bedside table and I knew my mom would get on the phone as soon as she heard my dad say my name. And I might need her as a buffer.

"I'm fine. I'm sorry to call so late, but I need some help."

"Jesus Christ," my dad muttered. I could hear the rustle of sheets and knew he was sitting up, his legs over the side of the bed, rubbing his face, turning on the bedside lamp.

It was not the first crisis call he'd gotten late at night. It wasn't even the first one from a daughter. It was just the first one from his do-no-wrong middle child.

"Lily, baby, are you sure you're okay?" my mom asked.

"She said she was fine, Susan." I knew that my father was

looking over his shoulder at her and they were staring across the bed at each other, both of them with a phone to their ear.

"A friend of mine did something stupid tonight and I was hoping you could, I don't know, maybe call someone here in Schoolport and see if there is anything you can do?"

"Is it Jane?" my father asked. Jane must have heard, because she stilled for just a moment, then continued on, this time going into our bathroom. Grabbing my damn toothbrush, I assumed.

"No, not Jane. Jane's actually in the room now, and we're all fine. It's for…this guy I've been seeing."

"Christ, Lily. A *boy*? What did he do?" There was a long-suffering sigh from him, like I asked for this kind of favor all the time.

"He…he stole a car. But it was—"

"What the hell? Why would a Bribury kid need to steal a car? Was it a joy-riding situation? A prank or something?"

"No, not like that. And he doesn't go to Bribury. He lives in Schoolport."

There was silence to that bit of news. "Just how good of friends are you with this boy?"

"I'm in love with him," I said with no hesitation. It was the strongest, the surest my voice had been since that girl had knocked on my door and told me Stick was waiting downstairs.

"But Lily, you just went out on one date with this boy for the first time last night," my mother said.

"That wasn't exactly the whole truth. Last night was our first date-date, but we've actually been…together for about six weeks."

"Jesus Christ. A campus full of boys with connections and you date a *townie*? And a car thief at that?"

"He's not really a car thief, it was a—"

"Yes, yes, he'd never done anything like it before, and would never do it again. They all say that, Lily."

It wouldn't be worth my breath to say that it was true in this case…at least about not doing it again.

I cleared my throat to make sure my voice didn't crack. "Will you help? I'm sure all it would take is one—"

"I know the DA in Schoolport well, Lily. You don't think I'd let you and Jane go to school in a town where I didn't have any connections, did you?"

The thought that he'd chosen my college based on DAs he could call if I was in trouble had never crossed my mind, but I suppose it should have.

No loose ends for Grayson Spaulding.

"I think this kid should just take what he gets, Lily. You can go on with your life and just—"

"But that's not what will happen," I said, drawing on my inner Spaulding. "What will happen is I will go over to his apartment and take care of his little brother while he's in jail. Because Lucas is Andy's guardian and raising him." I didn't need to add that their mother was still in the picture, hopeful she'd be able to stay in rehab until she was ready to be a fit parent to Andy.

I must have really sounded like a little Grayson, because Jane popped her head around the doorway to the bathroom and raised a brow at me, then did a silent golf clap in my direction.

"Not only do I love Lucas, but I'm very fond of his little brother, so if Lucas stays in jail, I'm going to take care of Andy. Which will probably mean a lot of missed classes, maybe even flunking out."

"Lily," my father said with warning in his voice.

"And I certainly won't be around the dorm to keep an eye on Jane. Who knows what she'll get into?"

Jane smiled at that and mouthed, "Burn!"

There was a moment of quiet. I could hear Stick's breathing as my father played out all his options in his head.

But I had him with the Jane thing, and I knew it.

"Okay, I'll make the call and get this kid out, as long as you're telling me the truth and it was just car theft and he doesn't have eight outstanding warrants or anything."

"He doesn't," I said. "Thank you, Dad. His name is Lucas Kade. Kade is spelled with a K."

I heard him write it down, the pencil scratching on paper. "But Lily, I will only make the call if you do something in return. That's how these things work, I know you know that."

I did. I'd grown up listening to my father—and mother, for that matter—making deals.

I thought he'd ask again for me to get Jane to stand in the wedding, and my heart sank, knowing there was no way Jane would do it, not even for Lucas. Not even for me.

But that wasn't his price. "You have to promise me, Lily, that if I get these charges dropped on this kid that you won't see him again. I can't take the risk of you being tied to him if it comes out that I stepped in. Let people just think…well, shit, I don't care what they think, but it can't be tied back to you."

"I…I…" My moment of victory was crashing around me. The thought of giving up Lucas making me breathless, hardly able to speak.

"Besides, clearly this boy isn't a good choice for you."

"But…Mom?" I said, hoping, pleading that she'd intervene on my behalf.

"I think your father has a good point, Lily. Obviously this boy, though you might love him, does not seem to be…good for you."

I thought of all the times I lay in Lucas's arms and felt strong, felt myself becoming the person I was meant to be. How could that not be good for me?

"But you don't—"

"It's a deal breaker, Lily," my father said.

"Okay," I said on a whisper, finding it painful to even breathe.

"Okay. I'll text you after I've spoken—"

"Wait. Wait. I need one more thing," I said.

"What's that?"

"I need to see Lucas one more time."

"Lily…"

"To break up with him in person. I have to do it in person. Anything else would be…cowardly."

"Okay," my father agreed, quicker than I would have guessed. "I admire you wanting to do that, Lily. And I admire your negotiating skills, young lady. We may have another Spaulding in the political arena yet."

"I don't think so," I said, and he just laughed, happy that a simple phone call was getting an undesirable boyfriend out of his daughter's life and discovering that she might be as politically savvy as himself.

Yeah, he was happy. And I was devastated.

"And Lily, I won't be able to know for sure that you've stopped seeing him. There are all kinds of ways around that. I'm taking you at your word."

I looked at Stick, and then at Jane, who had come all the way out of the bathroom. They'd been able to hear my parents' side of the conversation in the small room. I knew that from hearing countless conversations between Jane and her mother.

"You have my word," I said.

The phone call ended. I held my hand out to Stick for his phone, which he gave me. It was just like that first night when Lucas had taken my phone and called his phone with it. I did the same thing now. The noise of my phone ringing startled me, even though I'd just dialed it myself. I handed the phone back to Stick.

"Now you have my number. Call me when Lucas is out and we know for sure the charges have been dropped." He nodded. "And don't say anything to Lucas about what you just heard." He opened his mouth to protest. "I need to tell him myself."

"He's going to want to know why the charges were dropped."

I waved a hand. "You can tell him I called my father and he called the DA. Just don't tell him…the other."

He nodded, and placed a hand awkwardly on my shoulder. "That was well done, Lily, really."

"Yay, me," I said with absolutely no emotion. My feelings were going into shut-down mode, I could tell. Self-preservation. "If it's not cleared up by morning and Lucas isn't home by the time Mrs. Jankowski wakes up, call me and I'll go over there."

He nodded. "Got it." He squeezed my shoulder. "Nothing Basic about what you just did," he whispered in my ear, then kissed me on the cheek.

He nodded at Jane as he left. She nodded back, their claws for each other subsiding for the moment.

I went to my bed and sat on the edge. Jane dropped the bag she'd packed and came to sit beside me.

"You know you can totally still see him. Just do it on the sly, like your dad said."

I shook my head. "No, I can't. I gave my word."

She put her arm around me and pulled me close to her side.

"I know you can't," she whispered as I turned into her and started crying.

TWENTY-FIVE

Lucas

I KNEW what was coming. I'd known ever since Stick explained that just one call from Grayson Spaulding had made all my problems disappear.

Well, not all my problems. I still had one gigantic issue—how to hang on to Lily.

Stick had said she'd been magnificent with her father on the phone. It wasn't hard to imagine. Lily had a steely backbone that I don't think she even realized she possessed. Stick wouldn't give me any of the details of her conversation with her father. He said she wanted to talk with me about it herself.

So I waited a couple of days after I was released, hoping she'd call. Stick had called her when I got out, to let her know that her father had worked his magic.

And he must be quite the influencer, because I was home Sunday morning before Andy and Mrs. Jankowski were even awake. Nothing would show up anywhere, no record of any wrongdoing. I could only imagine the shit fit George Bell threw when he learned no charges would be filed against me.

A small salve to my otherwise shredded self-worth.

I was happy to realize that not once did I crave the escape of painkillers. It felt…*real* to feel the shame and all the other shitty feelings that were running through me.

So I let myself feel like shit and waited for Lily to call.

But she didn't.

On Tuesday, I wasn't sure whether I should be the one to take Andy to his swimming lesson or ask Stick to do it. I didn't want to piss Lily off by being there, or put her in an awkward position. But damn, I wanted to see her. The ache I felt at knowing I'd probably lost her was so much worse than when my shoulder blew apart. Because no surgery was going to fix this.

I ended up taking Andy to the lesson on Tuesday, and I watched from the spectator area, just like I had the first time I ever saw Lily.

She knew I was there, but she didn't catch my eye. No sly smiles, no sassy blown kisses like she'd done on one occasion.

Afterward, I waited in the hallway for Andy with the moms. They chatted a little bit with each other as we all waited for our kids. But I stayed apart, trying to think of something great to say to Lily when she brought Andy to me. Something so sterling that she'd have to stay with me.

I even thought about playing the "Andy needs you" card, but that wouldn't be fair—to either one of them.

Andy came out of the boys' locker room with Freddy and ran over to me. "I'm getting better, right, Lucas?" he said, looking up at me, anticipation—and adoration—on his little face.

Adoration I so obviously did not deserve.

"You bet you are. You're going to be swimming laps like Lily before you know it." He puffed up like a peacock and I placed my hand on his wet head.

I didn't know Grayson Spaulding, but I sent up a silent prayer of thanks to the man for allowing me to be there for Andy. To not have his life thrown off the rails any more than it already had been.

Lily came out with the little girls and two of them went over to Freddy, while the other two stayed with Lily.

"Let's go talk to Lily," Andy said, pulling on my hand.

"Wait a second, buddy. Let her talk with the mothers first.

We'll talk with her last."

He waited like a six-year-old, which is to say, not very patiently.

Finally everybody had cleared out except for the three of us. We moved to her side and she gave Andy a bright smile, while not meeting my eyes.

"And my favorite student! You did a great job today, Andy. I think next time you'll be able to float on your back without me holding you. Think so?"

He nodded his head, not quite enthusiastically, but not wanting to disappoint Lily, either.

Smart kid. I could tell him that disappointing Lily was one craptastic feeling.

"Can I talk with you for a minute?" she asked me. It was the first time she'd looked directly at me since I'd left her dorm room Saturday morning. Only four days ago, and yet an eternity. A lifetime.

"Of course," I said. We walked down the hall to one of the empty classrooms—the same one where she'd been upset about not having enough substance to write a paper on the person she was.

What a load of shit. She had more substance at eighteen than most forty-year-olds I knew.

"Andy, want to draw on the chalkboard while I talk with Lily for a second?" I said. He gave me a questioning look. Probably wondering if we were going to discuss his progress. "It's not about swim lessons. It's about something else."

His face turned to smug and knowing, and he nodded and turned, entering the classroom. I watched to make sure he was fine with drawing, then I shut the door. There was a window in it, so I'd be able to keep an eye on Andy as we stood in the deserted hallway. There wasn't much trouble he could get into in the old classroom, anyway.

"Lily," I said, then cleared my throat. Too much emotion was welling up and I wanted to be able to say my piece—state my case, such as it was—as objectively as I could.

"I said from the beginning I'm not what you need, Lily. But, God, I want to be. I want to try to be exactly what you need."

"Lucas—"

"And I know it sounds like bullshit, but you have to know I would never have stolen that car if there weren't…extenuating circumstances."

"Stick told me why you needed the money."

I nodded, panic rising in me. I so did not want to be the guy who made excuses for his mistakes. I wouldn't tell her that the car belonged to George Bell, Andy's father. What difference would it make, anyway? "Yeah. And, well, you just need to know that I realize what a stupid move it was, and in no way am I back in that life. I meant what I said to you…that's all in the past."

"I know," she said. No challenging, no questioning. And yet there was such a sadness in her voice that I knew it didn't matter what I said.

She was done with me. And I didn't blame her.

"Well…I don't know that there's anything left to say," I said, hoping—praying—I was wrong.

"Lucas, you need to know that, although we can't see each other anymore, it's not because of what you did Saturday night. Or at least not what *I* think about what you did."

What did that mean? On one hand she seemed to understand that George's Jag was a one-time deal and very—*very*—bad judgment on my part. It raised a glimmer of hope within me.

But she'd led with "even though we can't see each other anymore." Which were the words I had expected to hear today. And yet they still cut like a surgeon's scalpel.

"What *is* the reason we can't see each other?" But I was starting to guess. Grayson Spaulding was some kind of genius political strategist, and there was no way he was going to lift a finger unless there was something in it for him. "Your father," I said, so she wouldn't have to.

She nodded. She looked up at me, and I could see the tears

starting to gather in her beautiful eyes. "You need to know that I think you're exactly what I need. That I've never needed…never wanted…anyone like I have you."

"And I let you down."

She was shaking her head a little too emphatically. "No. You did what you felt you had to. It wasn't the right choice, but I can see how you felt it was the only choice." She swallowed, looking away for a second, then looked straight at me—as always, taking my breath away. "And I did too. Made the choice I felt was the right one."

I nodded. If she'd given me the choice Saturday night—stay in jail, incur a record that would jeopardize Andy's stability, or lose Lily—I probably would have made the same choice.

And it would have killed me as much as it was killing Lily.

I pulled her into my arms just as her tears spilled over. She clutched at me, and I wrapped her so tight I wasn't sure either of us would be able to breathe.

"Oh, Lucas," she said, her words muffled by my hoodie as she buried her head in my chest.

"You did the right thing. It sucks, and it's my fault. But… thank you. Thank you so much, Lily."

"Jane said I should just keep seeing you on the sly." She lifted her head from my chest, and looked up at me. The pain in her eyes rivaled mine, and I wished like hell I could take it for her. Bear it all myself. She sniffled and gave her head a tiny shake. "But I gave my word, you know? I can't go back on that. It was a deal I willingly made."

There was a tiny question in her voice, and it seemed like there could be a very small crack there, a tiny space for wiggle room where maybe I could spin it so Lily and I could still see each other.

But no, that was not the person Lily was. She might not know who she was yet, but I knew she was a person of honesty and integrity, and I did not want to be the one who crumbled that.

Shit, I wanted to emulate it.

"I know," I said, pulling her back into me, my hand in her glorious hair, holding her head into my chest again. "I know you gave your word, Lily. And I know you'll keep it. That's why I love you."

Her arms snaked around my waist, and we stood like that, her quietly crying, me doing my best not to.

Later, but not now. Now I could be strong for Lily, like she had been for me.

I gauged about the time when Andy would get bored and come barreling out of the classroom. Just before what I deemed that moment to be, I pulled away from Lily and wiped her tears away with my thumb.

I moved to kiss her, but stopped myself. What was the point? It would only remind me of the sweetness I would never again taste.

"I love you, Lucas," she whispered.

"I love you too," I said, taking my hands from her face, stepping away.

Proving my timing correct, Andy opened the door to the classroom and declared himself starving.

"Let's get you home and fed," I said, steering Andy away from the love of my life.

"See you Thursday," Andy called back to Lily. I saw the stricken look on her face at the thought of having to go through the pain of seeing each other—and yet not—two days from now.

"I'll have Stick bring him on Thursday, and both days next week," I said. Next week would be the last two sessions. I'd looked into more lessons for Andy next semester, but there would be nearly a month before those started up. And if Lily was one of the instructors, I'd have to rethink it entirely.

"Thanks," she said to the solution of Stick coming in my place for the last three lessons.

"And I'll be done with the steam room next week, too," I said.

She nodded. "Okay. I'm sure it will look great."

I shrugged. It would look great to me, but I thought it would seem like a lopsided tiling job to pretty much everybody else. Frank had approved my plan, though, and had been happy with my work thus far, so I was covered.

"This was your building first," I said, trying to make light in a moment that was breaking my heart.

And hers too, if her eyes were any indication. Though she put a tremulous smile on her face as she said, "You're damn right. You may have had it on loan, but that steam room is mine." Her voice wobbled at the last and she looked away. Then turned away.

"Bye, Lily," I said, and started walking away from her, Andy tagging along at my side, then dashing ahead of me.

"Goodbye, Lucas," I thought I heard her say, but I wasn't sure.

TWENTY-SIX

Lily

THE LAST day of swim lessons I thought Lucas might show up, but he kept his word and had Stick drop off Andy. The kids were really cute and so proud to show off the great strides they'd made during the ten-week program. For the last half-hour we just let them jump off the diving board, half of us instructors in the water if needed, the other half on the pool deck with the kids.

In a way, it was probably good that Lucas had indeed stayed away. I planned to keep my part of the deal I made with my father, but it had been so hard the day I told Lucas we had to stop seeing each other. And the pain hadn't lessened since. I'd started to text him several times, but had stopped myself. I almost had Jane wipe him from my contacts and texts—I couldn't seem to do it myself—but I didn't. Some masochistic part of me would pull up texts he'd sent and read them over and over.

Over the weekend, Syd, Jane, and I had gone to a few parties, and I'd tried to engage, tried to look at the Bribury guys with new and fresh eyes, but it hadn't worked. I only saw visions of Lucas sitting up in the spectator area watching me. Or flashes of his big and beautiful body over me, his hands in my hair, him whispering that he loved me.

Syd and Jane had pity on me, but I knew I was being a complete Debbie Downer. Yeah, we'd only been together seven weeks, and I had my whole college career—hell, my whole life—ahead of me. But Lucas was…*the one.*

On some level I knew I would go on. I would have college boyfriends. I would one day get married, and I'd love my husband. But I also knew with absolute certainty that I would never love anyone the way I loved Lucas Kade.

We gave out certificates of completion to the kids after the lesson, in the hallway with the mothers. Hugs were also given out to the kids, and I hung on to Andy a bit longer than his squirming six-year-old body would allow. He didn't get that I probably wouldn't ever see him again, and I didn't bring it up. Let Lucas handle that one. Or maybe Andy had enough going on in his life that not seeing Miss Lily again would be of little notice to him.

But I would notice. Beyond Lucas, I'd come to love little Andy. And I'd miss him.

Andy ran to show Stick his certificate, but Stick wasn't alone. Jane, apparently having just come into the building, was standing next to Stick. I waved goodbye to the rest of my kids and their mothers and made my way to Jane, who was looking at Andy's certificate, even though she'd never met him.

"Wow, great job, big guy," Jane said to Andy, who beamed up at her. Another victim to Jane's unexplainable orbit of attraction.

"What are you doing here?" I asked Jane at the same time Stick asked the same thing. Though his inflection was much more on "you" than mine on "here."

She shrugged, directing her answer to me, ignoring Stick. "I was on this side of campus and I thought I'd walk home with you." Much like the other time she'd shown up here unexpected—hoping to get a glance at the new guy I thought was so hot—I suspected she had been nowhere near the women's IM building. No, Jane knew today was the last day of lessons and that either Lucas would show, or he wouldn't, and either of those outcomes were bound to make the cut deeper.

A good friend, Jane. It just took a little doing to get past her prickly personality and become friends.

But on days like this, I was so glad I had.

I said another goodbye to Andy. He ran ahead of Stick, who turned to me and said, "I'm sure it doesn't help, but just know that he's as miserable as you look."

I nodded to him, understanding, and in a way appreciating the sentiment.

"Fuck you," Jane said to him. "She's doing just fine. And she looks amazing, thank you very much."

Stick looked at her, opened his mouth to answer, then just waved a dismissive hand at her. "Whatever," he said, and walked away, catching up with Andy, and they both left the building.

Jane looped her arm through mine and we turned back to the locker room. "No laps. Let's get you into dry clothes and go find somebody to get us some booze. I think we should get wasted tonight."

"Okay," I said half-heartedly. We entered the locker room and I went down my row to get my shower stuff. I peeled off my hoodie and yoga pants, and was still standing in my suit when I heard Jane's voice call from over the row of lockers, "So this is what the car thief does when he's not out boosting vehicles?"

I walked around the corner and saw that the tape had been removed from around the steam room. Lucas had thought he'd be finished this week. I hadn't looked around that corner when I'd arrived today, so hadn't noticed.

"Guess it's open for business," I said to Jane, though I still stood a bit away. Like, I don't know, Lucas might walk out of the room at any second, absurd as that idea was. And as desperately as I wished it to come true.

Jane rolled her eyes at me. "Come on. Don't be a pussy." She held the door open for me. I expected to see steam billowing out, but apparently nobody had turned it on. Probably because I was always the one to do that.

I walked in and looked around. Gone was the old teal tile of all one color and size. In its place was a mosaic of the ocean. He'd done something clever with the seating area so that, standing in the doorway, it had an almost 3-D effect of rolling waves crashing against uneven sand dunes and the black sky above.

Aquamarine and sea foam tiles mixed to create the swelling tide; irregularly cut pieces formed the tempestuous whitecaps of the waves. I stepped closer. It looked like the tiles creating the sand dunes were actually made of sand, but they were smooth when I placed a finger on them. A third of the upper seat and the wall were made up of midnight-blue and black tiles in an indiscernible pattern that looked chaotic close up, but spectacularly like a dark night's sky when taken as a whole.

That's the key, finding the art amongst all the crap, Lucas had said the night I tried to find art in the chaos of the graffiti wall. He had definitely found art in this small room.

"Pretty," Jane said. I didn't say anything. It was really beautiful, and vaguely familiar, though I couldn't say why. He and I had never gone to the beach together, but it almost felt like this was something he and I shared.

Sentimental crap, and I needed to snap out of it.

"He thought if he did a good job on this one, they'd give him some more special project work."

"I'd say there's a high likelihood of that happening. This is… well, let's just say his talents were wasted stealing cars."

"Jane," I said with warning in my voice. She held up her hands in surrender. I stepped away from the mosaic, to the doorway. I wondered if I should teach lessons next semester. If maybe I shouldn't just stay away from the women's IM building and instead swim laps at the other IM building.

And away from a constant reminder of Lucas.

We were silent on the walk home, and I appreciated Jane not trying to cheer me up. Saying goodbye to Andy and then seeing Lucas's finished work of art had my emotions spinning. As we walked into our room, I kicked off my Uggs and threw my fleece pullover in the general vicinity of my desk chair. I pulled my phone out of my backpack, setting it on my desk, and then my soggy clothes. After hanging my wet suit, yoga pants and hoodie on a hook, I pulled off my jeans and sweater, intending to get dressed for a night of revelry with Jane.

I stood in my panties and a camisole, both a pretty nude/peach color. I looked at my closet, bursting with Basic wear that would work for this evening. And then I looked at my bed, which I hadn't made this morning when I left.

The bed won. I went over and crawled in, sort of in the sheets, sort of on top of the comforter. "I think I'm going to just stay in tonight," I said to Jane, who was sitting on her bed, texting.

"If we stop partying, the terrorists win," she said without looking up from her phone.

"They've won…at least for tonight," I mumbled, my face in my pillow. I reached up and pulled the band out of my hair, letting the nearly dry mass tumble down my back. I knew it would be a wreck in the morning if I didn't get up and brush it, but I didn't have the energy to do even that. You'd have thought I'd swum double my laps, rather than none, as lethargic as I felt.

I heard a sharp intake of breath from Jane and looked over, expecting to see her staring at her phone screen with shock from the sound of her. But she was looking at me. Not so much at me, as in looking at my eyes or face, but at my body as a whole. "What?" I asked. But she just shook her head and continued to look over at me. "Is there, like, a bug on me or something?"

"No," she said softly. She put her head down, but then she looked over at me again, even squinted at me.

"What? You're freaking me out."

She shook her head and got off her bed. "Sorry, just zoned out for a second. You sure you don't want to go out?"

I turned my head back into my pillow. "No. But don't be going to any clubs in Chesney, either."

She laughed. "No worries. I'm going to zip over and see if Syd's around and wants to go. I'll be back to get dressed in a minute. Maybe you'll change your mind."

"I won't," I said, then heard the door to Syd's side of the suite open and close.

I didn't notice that she'd taken my phone with her.

I lay there and thought about Lucas and what I'd given up. And then I thought about how it had ultimately been the right choice. No matter how badly it hurt.

Sitting up in bed, I pulled my laptop over to me, quickly opening a blank Word doc before I lost my train of thought.

"As I write this today, the person I am is…" I began. My fingers began typing furiously. "Loyal and unique, although sometimes it takes seeing yourself through someone else's eyes to see that. And above all, I am strong. And I didn't realize it until I had to give up the thing I loved the most."

The damn thing nearly wrote itself, and I had to edit quite a bit to get it down to the assigned three thousand words.

TWENTY-SEVEN

Jane

"LILY? It's kind of late to be calling—are you okay?" Grayson Spaulding said when I called him using Lily's phone. Syd wasn't around, which was just as well. I sat on the forgotten Megan's bed.

"Mr. Spaulding. This isn't Lily. This is…Jaybird Winters," I said, using the name I gave up in seventh grade, demanding everyone call me Jane. I had it legally changed to Jane at fifteen.

"Jaybird? Jane?" Yep, that got his attention. "Is Lily okay?"

"Lily's fine. I just borrowed her phone."

A pause, then: "To what end, Jane?"

No wonder my dipshit of a father kept Spaulding close…he was one shrewd SOB. Emphasis on SOB.

"I'm aware of the deal you and Lily made a couple of weeks ago."

Nothing.

"And I'd like to make a deal of my own with you."

"I'm listening," he said after a moment's pause.

"I want you to let Lily out of her deal and allow her to see Lucas."

"Why would I want to do that?"

"Isn't your daughter's happiness reason enough?"

"No." No pause or anything. Suddenly, growing up with an absentee father didn't seem so bad.

"Okay. If her happiness means nothing to you—"

"Which is not what I said, and you know it."

I smiled. I kind of liked talking to the man who had always held my father's strings. "Well, if Lily being miserable, and Lucas actually being a pretty decent guy who loves your daughter, won't change your mind, then how about…" I waited for emphasis. I hadn't been raised by the ultimate drama queen for nothing.

"Yes?"

"How about if I agree to stand in Betsy's wedding?" Ooh, that had him thinking.

"You would do that? Lily said there was no way she could talk you into doing it."

"She was right. She couldn't have. But let's just say I have recently seen…how much Lucas and Lily belong together. And I feel strongly enough about it to make this call and offer myself up as the sacrificial lamb."

"Standing in a wedding is hardly a huge sacrifice."

"Don't kid yourself. It's going to be hell, and not just on that day, but in the photos that will live on forever."

There was a pause, and then a deep exhale. I could almost hear his political mind weighing the pros and cons at lightning speed. "If I agree, you have to actually…*behave* at the wedding. No all-day pouting, no dramatics. You need to act like you're happy to be there."

"I—"

"You don't have to hang all over the bride and groom with fake happiness or anything like that. But no 'I can't believe I have to fucking be here' faces, either."

This man knew me well. But that wasn't news to me.

"Okay. But for the 'no pouting faces' I want assurances that when you tell Lily she can see Lucas, you make sure she can do it guilt-free. No 'I'm still against you seeing him, but if you really must, I won't stand in your way' or some such bullshit."

He laughed. Grayson Spaulding actually laughed.

"I mean it. You tell her that—"

"I think I can manage to make her believe that I changed my mind…Jaybird."

I smiled. I had gotten his goat, and now he'd gotten mine. I really did kind of like the dick. "Do we have a deal?" I asked.

"Deal."

"I'll call my father and tell him I changed my mind about the wedding as soon as Lily and Lucas are back together. And one more thing—I don't want Lily to know about this call. Let her think you just changed your mind…because you *do* care about her happiness."

"Fine."

I hung up and went back into our room. Lily was sitting up in bed, banging away on her laptop. So engrossed with what she was doing she didn't even notice when I placed her phone back on her desk before going to my closet to find something to wear for the night.

TWENTY-EIGHT
:::

Lily

ARE YOU *available to talk? And are you alone? (or at least no Lucas),*
I texted to Stick the Monday after the last swim lesson.

A moment later, he answered yes to both, and I called him.

"Do you know Lucas's boss, Frank?" I asked him.

"Yeah. He's from the neighborhood. He's, like, my dad's age,
so it's not like we're buds or anything, but yeah, I know him.
Why?"

"Think he'd do a favor for you?"

"Hell no, he hates my guts."

I was going to ask if Stick had stolen Frank's car, but decided
not to. I needed him. "Think he'd do a favor for Lucas?"

"Hell yes, L is Frank's boy."

"Great. Here's what I want to happen…"

I told Stick my plan and gave him exact instructions on day
and time for it all to go down.

"I thought your dad made—"

"Things have changed," I said.

A small pause and then Stick said, "Well, thank Christ. I don't
think I could have stood his melancholy ass too much longer."

"So, you're pretty sure he would want to…see me again?"

Stick's snort of disbelief sounded like Beethoven to my ears.
"Uh…that would be a yes."

"Because I can just leave it alone…" The idea of being able to date Lucas but him already having moved on was devastating. But I knew that, regardless of Stick's answer, I was going to see my plan through. The "person I am today" was someone who was brave and followed her heart.

"Don't leave it alone. Make your play."

"Thanks, Stick," I said. I was about to hang up when I added, "Not so Basic now, am I?"

He laughed. "There was never anything Basic about you, Lily," he said, and then hung up.

And I started thinking about tomorrow night.

TWENTY-NINE
❖

Lucas

I HADN'T expected to be back in the women's IM building so soon. And certainly not in the women's locker room. Frank and I had discussed redoing the men's locker room at some point, but I was already working on a tile mural project in the admin building as of Sunday night.

But Frank had called at midnight and said there was an issue with the tiles in the steam room, and for me to go over and see what was wrong.

I felt a little bit of panic. I was sure I had done all the sealants correctly. Used the right kind of adhesive for the steam. Hopefully whatever it was could be fixed quickly and something I could do on my own. I did not want my first solo project to be something somebody else had to come in and fix.

The lights in the locker room were off, and I flicked them on. When I turned the corner, I could see that the lights to the steam room were already on. I opened the door and a billow of steam met me. Shit. Somebody had used it earlier tonight and left the heater on. It would take a while to cool it down so I could take a good look at the tile. I wondered if it had been Lily who had used it, but she said she was always very careful about turning it off before she left. Turning to leave and shut off the heater, I saw movement out of the corner of my eye. Somebody was in here.

"Oh, I'm so sorry. I was just—" The steam had cleared just enough for me to make out the gorgeous naked body laid out on my tile job. It was the mosaic's inspiration herself. "Lily?"

She turned her head and looked at me. She was lying on a towel on her stomach, her head resting on her folded arms. Looking exactly like she had in her bed the day I came up with idea for the steam room. "I didn't know you'd be here," I said, trying to call up all my self-control and not go over and run my hands down her glistening, sleek body. "I'm sorry. I'll leave you—"

"You don't have to leave," she said, stopping me. "I don't *want* you to leave."

She was going to break the deal with her father. I could be strong for the both of us and leave, give her time to think this through. I knew moments of weakness, for sure, but I did not want to be a moment of weakness for Lily that she'd regret later.

"I think it'd be better if I left."

Her body tensed. I could see it in the long line of her back. But she stayed where she was, emulating the scene that she lay upon. "I won't stop you if you *want* to leave," she said, and I almost laughed at that ridiculous thought. "But you need to know that my father changed his mind and has given me his blessing to see you."

My breath, barely recovered from seeing a gloriously naked Lily, left me altogether. "I…I…"

"So it's up to you, Lucas." She picked up a water bottle from in front of her and tossed water onto the steam mechanism, sending a flare of new steam out from the bottom of the walls. "Can you stand the heat?" she asked, and then she rolled to her side and placed a hand on her hip, challenging me.

My clothes were off in seconds, thrown out into the locker room, the door closed, and I was sitting on the towel she was lying on, gathering her in my arms. Christ, to feel her soft, pliant arms go around my neck again when I thought I'd never even *see* her again?

She slid a leg over my lap and sat facing me, straddling me.

"Lily," I whispered, skimming my hands along her hips, pulling her closer against me. I looked into her eyes, questioning.

"Yes," she whispered, then softly pressed her lips against mine. "It's real. And it's okay." I put my hands on her face, along her jaw, and kissed her with all the stinging pain that I'd felt over the last two weeks. Devouring her as the darkness without her had devoured me.

"I can't believe it," I said between kisses. She wrapped her arms tightly around my neck, her tits smashing into my chest, her tongue darting into my mouth, finding mine.

"Believe it," she said against my lips.

I wanted to drag it out. I wanted to lay her back down on the tile and lick every steamy inch of her body. I needed to touch and touch some more just to convince myself that she wasn't some mirage brought on by the heat of the steam room.

But Lily had other ideas. She pulled her arms from around me and ran her hands down my chest, sitting back just enough to make room. As she nuzzled my neck, licking here and there to my ever-growing cock's delight, her hand snaked down and wrapped around me. She moved up to her knees, and I was thankful she'd had the forethought to put a towel down on the beautiful—but very hard—tile.

And although my thinking was getting very hazy as she guided me to her and then eased down on me, the realization that this had all been planned—and well planned, involving Frank—zipped through me.

"This is perfect," I said as she lifted herself a tiny bit, then slid back down on me. I grasped her perfect ass and she put her hands on my shoulders, her fingers digging into me. "That you picked this place, and laid out like that." I gasped as she rose higher and came down harder. "So fucking perfect."

She licked her lips, beads of sweat running down the side of her face. I leaned forward and licked a drop off her jaw. "I didn't see it at first," she said.

"What do you mean?" On this downward movement of her

hips, I held her in place and ground her down on me, tilting her so her clit got some good friction. Her gasp proved I found the right spot. I ground again, and she leaned forward and nipped at my throat, then licked where she'd bitten.

"Fuck, Lily," I moaned. I wouldn't be able to hold on; it was too damn much to have her back in my arms, to be buried deep inside her, when I'd thought I'd never see her again. "God, I love you," I said, and I flexed my hips to meet her strokes.

"Me…too," she got out on breathy sighs as she rode me. Her tits jiggled, and I used one hand to guide a breast to my eager mouth as my other hand dug into her ass, coaxing her to go faster.

Which she did, even though it was the end of me. I tried to hold back, make it last, but it was impossible. When I felt that I was just about to explode, I reached around and stroked her clit, willing her to come with me. I looked into her eyes and I didn't even have to say the words. She gave me a small nod of understanding, a soft kiss, and then her head fell back and her body started convulsing with her climax. I was right behind her, holding her tight as both of our bodies were racked with spasms of pleasure.

And love.

"What did you mean? Earlier, when you said you didn't see it at first?" I asked her later. We were still in the steam room, and she was still in my arms. God, I was afraid to let her go, I just couldn't believe that she was mine again.

"The steam room design. I didn't see that it was…me." She looked uncertain all of a sudden. "It *is* me, right? Like, in my bed?"

I stroked her back. Her skin was so slick with moisture my hands almost slid off her body. "Yes, it's you. Though I couldn't really do you as I wanted to. I had to keep it abstract enough that nobody would realize it was a naked woman. No nips showing or anything."

She swatted playfully at my shoulder. Then ran her hand

along my neck and to the back of my hair, tangling her fingers in what was probably a soaking rat's nest by now. "Yeah. No. I didn't see it. Jane was the one who recognized the similarities."

"Well, I suppose she and I are the only ones who have seen you naked on your bed. You wouldn't know what a goddamned beautiful sight you are like that." I looked her up and down. "Or like this."

She smiled at me. "I love you, Lucas."

I kissed her. She tasted like...a beautiful second chance.

EPILOGUE

Lily

"NICELY DONE, Ms. Spaulding," Montrose said as he handed me my graded paper. I'd scored a ninety-three on it. He'd written "Overly sentimental, but great flow" in the margin.

Yes, that kind of summed up my first semester as a Bribury freshman: overly sentimental, but definitely a great flow. And I was just fine with that.

It was the Friday before our three-week holiday/semester break. I would spend the first week with Lucas in Schoolport, then go home to DC for the rest. My parents weren't crazy about those plans, but they'd be at Betsy Stratton's wedding next weekend anyway, so they didn't fight it too much.

I could have gone to the wedding with my parents if I'd wanted to, but Jane had forbidden it. "There's no way I'm going to be able to put on the fakiest fake fakery if you're around. So please, just let me bear this day from hell alone." I had quickly agreed, not really wanting to be there.

I never outright asked Jane if she'd offered up her bridesmaid acceptance to my father in exchange for him letting me out of our deal. I'd hinted at it once, and she'd just given me a blank look and said she didn't know what I was talking about.

I'd let it go. But I was eternally grateful.

Lucas was going to take the train to DC a couple of days after

Christmas and stay with us so we could be together on New Year's Eve. He was cutely nervous about meeting my parents. I was sure my dad would put him through the wringer, but once he and my mom saw how much Lucas and I loved each other…Well, okay, they may still not be very happy about the idea, but it didn't really matter much.

"Well, boys and girls, it has indeed been a pleasure," Montrose said from the front of the room, all the papers dispersed. "You have made what I thought was going to be hell on earth a rather enjoyable experience." There was laughter in the small classroom. Montrose looked pointedly at Jane and added, "Well, *most* of you, anyway." She smirked back at him. I looked to see what she'd received on her paper, but she'd already folded it. I did see a lot of red ink fading through the last page.

"Thank you, and have a happy holiday," he said, and motioned that we were dismissed. It was about twenty minutes early. Lucas was picking me up on this side of campus and we were going to go Christmas shopping for gifts for his family this afternoon. I had no other classes today, and Jane was leaving campus later today when her mom picked her up, so Lucas and I would have the dorm room to ourselves all night and all day tomorrow before students had to be out of the dorm for break on Sunday.

His mom had been home from rehab for a couple of weeks, and I'd met her a few times. She seemed to be doing well, but I hadn't known her before, so I didn't have anything to compare it to.

Lucas said he was optimistic, though. He was staying at the apartment with her and Andy for the time being, which was probably good for all of them. Though for the week I was still in town, he and I would be staying in the apartment he had shared with Stick.

The money issues that had driven Lucas to the extreme of stealing a car had been resolved. Lucas hadn't wanted to talk about it, but I had pressed, wanting to make sure he hadn't done anything stupid.

He said that Andy's father had ponied up the money for Lucas's mother's extended rehab stay and a few months of rent. He'd also signed away all rights to Andy and paid for the legal fees that made Lucas Andy's guardian if his mom wasn't able to take care of Andy.

I asked what had made Andy's father show up out of the blue and offer at least money—if no other kind of support or interest in getting to know his son.

Lucas had shrugged and said, "I guess his conscience had a wake-up call. Like…some *alarm* went off for him or something." He'd smiled at that, some kind of private joke. I let it go.

I gathered up my bag, and as the three of us walked to the door, Montrose called after us, "Ms. Winters, Ms. O'Brien, may I see you both, please?"

All three of us exchanged glances and invisible shrugs. "Maybe he's thinking three-way," Jane whispered, and Sydney jabbed her with an elbow. By the clearing of his throat, I guessed that Montrose had heard her. Which was probably exactly the way Jane wanted it.

"I'll see you guys at the room later?" I asked. We had planned on exchanging our gifts to each other this afternoon before Jane's mom showed and Syd caught the train to New York.

"Sounds good," Syd said, and she and Jane walked over to Montrose's table/lectern area. I wanted to stick around, but I knew I'd get all the juicy details later from them both.

Besides, my man was waiting for me outside.

I nearly floated out of Bailey Hall and saw him across the parking lot. His pose was similar to that night we'd looked at the graffiti wall as he leaned against the blue car Stick had lent him. I went and stood next to him, my butt against the cold metal of the car. Together, we faced the front of Bailey Hall.

"No boobs and penises on this wall," he said, and I knew he was remembering that night as well. He slung an arm around me, and I nestled my head against his chest, happy to stay like this for a while, even though it was cold enough to be snowing, which it probably would later.

I thought about the stark differences of our "walls"—his covered in illegal graffiti, mine covered in tasteful brick and ivy. It could be said that it symbolized the differences in Lucas and me. But both walls were beautiful in their own way.

And both were strong and sturdy, and would stand the test of time.

Somehow, I knew that Lucas and I would too.

~*~

Acknowledgements

I would like to thank Taylor Kearly for bringing me up to speed on certain aspects of a college freshman's life and vernacular. And especially the term "Basics" which I borrowed and embellished for my own literary purposes.

May you have an awesome freshman year, Taylor, but stay away from those badboy townies!

The Freshman Roommates Trilogy
continues with Jane's story in

Mara Jacobs is the *New York Times* and *USA Today* bestselling author of The Worth Series

After graduating from Michigan State University with a degree in advertising, Mara spent several years working at daily newspapers in advertising sales and production. This certainly prepared her for the world of deadlines!

She writes mysteries with romance, thrillers with romance, and romances with…well, you get it.

Forever a Yooper (someone who hails from Michigan's glorious Upper Peninsula), Mara now splits her time between the Copper Country and Las Vegas.

You can find out more about Mara's books at
www.marajacobs.com

Mara loves to hear from readers. Contact her at
mara@marajacobs.com

Made in the USA
Monee, IL
18 August 2024

64099899R00125